All

Our

Squandered

Beauty

Praise For Amanda Huggins

"Reading Amanda Huggins is like taking a journey around the world. Her stories are so beautifully written we forget where we are. Japan, Russia, Paris, London, the States, we are drawn into a series of fascinating lives. Hearts are broken but survive, scuffed and painted bright colours, people never fail to keep trying. These are stories we need to read."

- Angela Readman, author of
Something Like Breathing.

"Amanda Huggins has created a masterclass in short fiction with *Scratched Enamel Heart.* Whether the story is one page or ten, every one is an exemplar of the craft. Readers will be left thinking about choice and freedom, love and grief, sacrifice and self-preservation; and the book stands up exceptionally well to repeated reading. Huggins is definitely an author to watch."

- Amanda McLeod, author of *Animal Behaviour* and Managing Editor at Animal Heart Press.

"Amanda writes with empathy, an eye for vivid detail, and a sense of adventure. Her stories display darkness and light, vulnerability and strength, and great charm."

- Alison Moore, author of the Booker-shortlisted novel
The Lighthouse.

"Huggins is a highly accomplished writer who uses language both beautiful and at the same time sparing, there are no indulgent passages of prose to detract from the main message. Every word is weighed before inclusion. A delight."

- Sandra Danby, author of *Connectedness.*

All

Our

Squandered

Beauty

Amanda Huggins

Victorina Press
www.victorinapress.com

Typesetting and Layout: Jorge Vasquez
Cover design © Triona Walsh
Cover partly based on
original artwork 'Inside the Sea' © Amanda Huggins

British Library Cataloguing in Publication Data
A catalogue record for this book is available from the
British Library.

ISBN: 978-1-8380360-6-5

Typeset in 12pt Garamond
Printed and bound in Great Britain by 4edge ltd.

To live in hearts we leave behind
Is not to die

- Thomas Campbell

ONE

A squabble of seagulls took flight, startled by the sound of a distant siren. Kara and Louise watched them swoop and wheel in the fading light, circling the lighthouse, crowding the sky, as though trapped inside a giant snow globe.

The girls turned back at the end of the pier, aware of the siren growing louder, watching the flashing blue light as it moved towards them around the curve of the bay. Kara spotted a group of people at the top of the steps. She heard the urgency in their voices, became aware of the smack of the sea against the harbour wall. Through the legs of the crowd she made out two men crouched next to a prone figure, a young woman, jeans leaden with water, a cheesecloth shirt wound around her torso like a wet bandage. A spaniel circled the group frantically, coat plastered to his ribs, the gleam of his butterscotch fur darkened and dulled by seawater.

Lou pushed forward to ask what was happening, but Kara didn't follow. She stumbled against the herring sheds, folding in on herself, hardly noticing the pools of brackish water, the smell of rotting fish. She caught only snatches of Louise's conversation with the group, but it was enough to work out what had happened. The dog had slipped off the steps into the sea, the woman had overbalanced trying to save him.

The ambulance pulled up on the pier and Kara heard the woman's spluttering gasps as she coughed up saltwater. She felt the stir of old memories, as though dredged from the ocean floor, a still-bright film playing on a loop inside her head. The tug of the relentless tide, a certainty that the world was nothing but sea – no sky, no rock, no earth, just the blue and grey and green of the water. She remembered the ache of her muscles, arching her feet as though she were a ballet dancer, reaching down and down, trying to touch the seabed with her toes. She felt the weight of water close over her, the crash and rush of wave and spume, clouded with churning sand. No sight of land or horizon, only endless sea. The feeling of elation, the sure knowledge that the tide would take her to Da. Then the gulp as she surfaced, breathing half-air, half-water before she disappeared again beneath the waves, powerless against the force of the currents.

When Kara registered the voice, it came from somewhere distant, as though she were still underwater, and she shook her head like a dog dislodging water from its ears.

'Are you okay? They're taking the woman to hospital, just to be sure, but she'll be fine.'

She looked up and saw one of the trawler lads standing in the shed doorway, his hand reaching down for hers. As he pulled her up she met his steady gaze, saw something reassuring in his dark eyes – a solid promise. Kara felt she already knew him, as if they were ex-lovers or blood brothers, as if he understood something about her she hadn't yet worked out for herself.

'Yes, I'm alright, thanks. It just shook me up a bit.'

'I'm Jake,' he said. 'Jake Andrews. Just moved into one of the cottages up at Elmwick Bay. I've seen you around with the bikers. I've got a motorbike myself, but I haven't really had a chance to get to know anyone in Hayborough yet.'

'You're not from here originally then?'

'No, I'm from up the coast. Ravengrove. Pirate country.'

He half-laughed as he said it, checked her expression as though expecting a judgement. She smiled, looked him up and down.

'And is this what swashbuckling buccaneers look like in 1978? Jeans and fishing aprons instead of jaunty hats and feisty parrots?'

He laughed again and she blushed. 'Sorry, Jake, I've got to go now, my friend will be waiting for me.'

'Hope to see you again then, er . . .?'

'Kara. Yeah, you too.'

As she turned around, the ambulance pulled away and she saw Lou standing at the other side of the pier. It was almost dark now, lights were reflected in the water like scattered cinders, halyards clinked gently against a jumble of masts. They linked arms as they walked back around the harbour together and Kara was grateful when Lou didn't question her, didn't ask why she'd held back from the crowd on the pier.

They ordered coffees in Charelli's and sat up at the counter on high stools. The new single by The Stranglers was playing on the jukebox, almost drowned out by the rattle and ding of the pinball machine. A few of the biker crowd were chatting in the booths at the back, and when the waitress turned away they tipped nips of whisky into their coffee from hip flasks tucked inside their leathers.

3

Louise blushed when Davy Black spoke to her on his way out.

'Come down to the arcade in the morning, Lou? Mind you do, darling, I need you as my good-luck charm when I'm playing the bandits.'

'You're not going are you?' Kara asked. 'What about Paul?'

'Of course I'm not going – but it's nice to be asked. Who was that I saw you talking to on the pier?'

'Some lad from Ravengrove. Jake, I think he said. He lives in Elmwick now.'

'A sevener? You want to watch yourself there, Kara Bradshaw. Those fishermen's lads from Raven are as wild as they come. I think he's the one who lost his brother in a car accident.'

'Why do they call them seveners anyway?'

Louise shrugged. 'Don't ask me. You're usually the expert on all that sort of stuff. It's to do with some traditional sea ritual I think?'

As the door clattered shut behind Davy and his friends, Kara looked up and watched them walk past the window. The boy at Davy's side was Alfie Machin. He'd been in her class at Elmwick Primary, then he'd moved up to the sea training school here in Hayborough. Kara felt her cheeks redden as their eyes met, wondered if he'd say anything to his friends about Da, if he'd point her out as he talked to them behind his hand. Her mam always said that stories soon grow stale, people move on and look for something new to gossip about. Yet Kara had never been sure. Even though seven years had passed, everyone in the fishing community knew of Ged Bradshaw and they still had unanswered questions.

Seven years. To Kara, it sounded like forever. For the first ten years of her life she and Da had been inseparable; now seven whole years had passed without him being there. Sometimes she thought of those years as a road stretching back into the distance, the white lines stitching it in place. It was as though she were joined to her past by a long silver thread that lengthened day by day. As the thread uncoiled it tightened, and she was terrified that one day it would snap.

When they left Charelli's, Kara fell silent, shaking her head when Louise asked if anything was wrong. Yet as soon as they parted at the corner of Eastgate, she felt the tears well up. Kara never let anyone see her cry, particularly her mam, who'd have her sent back to the doctors to answer a hundred questions all over again.

'See you Monday morning at 8.30,' Lou yelled. 'I'll call you tomorrow night so we can coordinate our packing.'

Kara wiped her eyes on her sleeve and turned round.

'It's only three days in London, Lou, not two weeks on the Costa Brava.'

'Well we still want to look our best!' she shouted.

Kara saw the last bus turning into the stand and ran across the road. The driver was Allen Dixon, her boyfriend's cousin, and she perched on the seat across from his cab and talked to him as they pulled out of town.

'Marty says you're going on a college trip next week?'

She nodded. 'Yeah, it's the lower sixth art trip to London.'

'Well don't you go flirting with those fancy southern boys and forget about us Yorkshire lads,' he said, laughing.

Kara shook her head. 'As if I would!'

She jumped off the bus at the top of Milestone Hill, opposite the narrow lane that led down to High Rigg farmhouse.

'Take care of yourself, Kara,' called Allen as the doors hissed shut.

When the lights of the bus disappeared around the bend, she saw the night sky clearly, black as sea coal, scattered with fistfuls of stars. She looked for the moon, but it was only a fledgling crescent; barely a fingernail clipping of light. When the sound of the bus faded into the distance, there was an uneasy rustle across the moor: the dull thud of a clumsy ewe stumbling in the dark, the soft baa of a half-grown lamb, the whisper of unseen life in the cow parsley and oxeye daisies spilling out across the lane. The farmhouse was set back in a shallow dip, clinging to the hillside for shelter, out of sight until Kara rounded the last bend in the track. Yet she was never apprehensive of the walk after dark, hardly ever thinking to use the small torch she carried in her bag.

They'd lived at High Rigg since she was eleven. After Da's accident the cottage in Elmwick Bay had been sold to pay off the mortgage, and within a year Kara and Mam had moved into the farmhouse to take care of her grandmother for the last few months of her life. Granny Eileen had always lived on the farm even though she'd been widowed just before Kara was born. Her grandfather's prize sheep herd was sold to their neighbours, the Reids, and the land had been rented to them ever since.

When she rounded the bend, Kara saw Mam had left the porch light on for her. She knew Pilot was in the yard before she opened the gate. She could hear his quiet whine, his claws clicking on the flagstones as he paced back and forth outside his kennel. She unclipped his lead, let him slip in through the door at her side and follow her up the narrow stairs to the attic.

She undressed quickly and climbed straight into bed. Pilot jumped up and flopped down at her side, his head resting on her foot. Yet she couldn't settle. When she closed her eyes she saw Alfie Machin laughing outside Charelli's window, the pale face and knotted hair of the woman who'd almost drowned. She remembered the gurgle of her lungs as she coughed up seawater, could feel a tightness in her own chest. Kara opened her eyes again, straining to catch the distant murmur of the waves, but the wind wasn't blowing in the right direction. Although she was no more than a mile from the shore, up at High Rigg she might as well have been fifty.

She wriggled her foot free from underneath the soft weight of Pilot's head, climbed out of bed and opened the window wide, sliding out to sit on the flat roof for a while, her back resting against the cool stones of the chimney. In the daytime she could see the sea from here, a distant expanse of blue, but at night the horizon merged into the sky. She remembered sitting on her window seat at the cottage in Elmwick Bay, listening to the gentle lap of the water, the shouts of the fishermen as they said their goodnights and headed home from the pub.

Kara missed the sea view from her bedroom

almost as much as she missed Da. He'd prepared the room for her before she was even born, painting the walls soft grey and duck-egg blue, transforming the ceiling into a midnight sky filled with stars created from handfuls of sequins. When she outgrew her cot he created a deep bunk bed with a mock porthole above it, like the inside of a ship's cabin. Underneath he built a desk. He found old posters of shellfish, seaweed, coastal flowers, and pinned them to the wall. He made a high window seat with steps leading up to it, concealing a secret compartment at its base where Kara hid her most treasured possessions. From the outside the panel looked smooth and flat, yet a small door sprang open if you pressed gently at one end.

She would sit in the window for hours, looking out across Elmwick Bay at nothing but sea and sky, and in the early morning the pale eastern light would stream in through the salt-stained glass.

And although Kara loved the lights and cafes and arcades of Tayborough's seafront, the open moorland above High Rigg, the wheeling lapwings and the coconut scent of gorse flowers in spring, she missed the raw beauty of Elmwick, the familiarity of every rock pool and current, knowing the names of all the boats and the faces of all the fishermen.

When she crawled back under the covers, Pilot flopped down across her legs. The solid heft of him was reassuring, just like the weight of Da when he'd sat at the foot of her bed. Every night he read her the stories of the Japanese sea gods, Ebisu and Nakatsutsu, the fairy tales and myths of the ocean, of sea serpents and sirens. And her favourite tale of all, the tale of Sakara, the guardian sea sprite from *Stories of the Northernmost Sea*, after whom she'd been named. When she'd tried to read the books for herself, she discovered it was Da who had brought the words to life, and without his way of storytelling they held little magic. Sometimes, Mam had told her folktales of her own. But her stories never shone. There were no mermaids or dolphins or sea sprites in them; they were inland stories of wolves and goblins.

Whenever Da wanted Kara to go to sleep, he listed the names of seaweed and the collective nouns for birds, as soporific as a lullaby. Now they merged into one as she recited them in her head: a convocation of murlins, a clamour of purple claw, a confusion of spiny straggle and a charm of oyster thief, a kettle of sugar kelp and a scold of landlady's wig, a mob of hairy basket, a gaggle of dabberlocks, a deceit of devil's tongue.

When she finally fell asleep she dreamt about Da for the first time in weeks, and in her dreams they inhabited the sea together as though they were fish. They swam away from his boat, down and deep through shoals of glittering herring, and they were smiling. But at dawn she was alone again, run aground without him.

TWO

Just before noon on Sunday, Kara heard the growl of Marty's motorbike. She snatched up her helmet and leather jacket, dashing outside to meet him in the yard. She didn't want him to know that Mam was out.

When Marty told Kara he loved her, she said it straight back without much thought as to what the words really meant. He was kind and thoughtful, she liked having him around, yet he didn't make her heart stop or share her dreams, and he could never provide the security she craved. However much he said he loved her, Marty's affection would always be conditional, and Kara needed something more solid than the fair-weather love of a nineteen-year-old boy. But he'd been there last summer at the right moment, in that hopeful gap between school and sixth form college when it felt as though the real future was finally beckoning.

Lou and Kara had spent that long hot summer chasing boys, wasting days as though they had forever, idling away their afternoons on the boating lake and in the smoke-haze of the foreshore arcades. At the lake they'd flirted with the lads staying at the caravan park, down from Glasgow for the annual factory shutdown. They purposely drifted alongside the boys' rowing boats, tangling their oars together, all helpless giggles, cheesecloth shirts tied up to reveal the caramel skin of their taut stomachs. In the late afternoons they'd head across to the arcades, strutting and pouting in front of the rake-limbed lads fresh out of sea training school. The boys were making the most of a few weeks of freedom before they started their working lives on the trawlers. They acted confident and cool, admiring their reflections in the mirrored walls, combing their hair, rolling up their shirt sleeves to reveal new tattoos: hearts and skulls, swallows and anchors, declarations of love. Lou and Kara would go over to ask them for a light, their voices half drowned out by the jangle and blare of the slot machines. They held their cigarettes up high, elbows cupped in their opposite hands like 1940s film stars, tapping the ash onto the stained red carpet, never inhaling. They posed, hands on hips, all flirt and glance, eyes half-closed with the want of something they barely understood.

And when they'd tired of the trawler lads and the tourists, they pursued the bikers who met up in Charelli's coffee bar. They'd cadge a lift to the pub up on the moors, riding pillion through the woods with boys they hardly knew, or piling inside someone's Dolomite or Granada, racing through country lanes with the windows down. The girls sat on the boys' knees, their heads almost touching the vinyl roof. They turned up the music as loud as they could, to show the world how reckless they were, to amplify life, to feel their speed. And at every bend there was a moment when the car might leave the ground, might flip into the ditch or fly through the air. But no one cared, no one could imagine being anything but alive, free, hurtling into the night with pure joy coursing through their veins. Even though they'd lost friends in accidents, they themselves were surely invincible, too fast to live and too young to die.

One Saturday night, at the height of that long, lazy summer, Kara went home on the back of Marty Lowe's Bonneville. When he reached the woods he turned off into the trees, riding slowly down the narrow track until they were hidden from the road. She hadn't known him long; he was a friend of Louise's new boyfriend, Paul. Yet she said nothing when he laid out his jacket on the soft pine needles, didn't resist when he kissed her and slipped his hand between the buttons of her denim shirt. She felt the heat from the Bonneville's engine, heard the tick of it cooling, inhaled Marty's scent – lemon soap and engine oil – and knew she was ready to try this out. She wanted it. She wanted him because he wanted her, wanted what came after that flutter of excitement she felt when men looked at her in a certain way.

And as she lay there, she thought of the waiter at the hotel she'd worked in during last year's holidays, recalled the heat of that bleached-out summer of 1976, remembered the night he pressed his body against hers under the Luna Park boardwalk. The warmth of the air, the smell of chips and candy floss, the pure white of his shirt against the tan of his arm, the feel of his hips moving against hers, the give of him, the hardness of him, her forehead resting against his shoulder. That feeling of something slipping and melting inside her that was so beautiful she wanted to hold on to it forever. And she thought of him still as Marty Lowe pushed inside her, cried out at the short, sharp pain, and said 'yes' very quietly when he asked if she'd enjoyed it.

When he dropped her off at the top of Milestone Hill she ran down the lane with her heart thudding, crept upstairs so Mam wouldn't ask where she'd been, wouldn't see that she looked different. She combed the woods out of her hair, hardly noticing the things that fell from it: the dead moth, the nubs of twigs, the handful of pine needles she found scattered on her bedroom floor the next morning. She pushed her blood-stained knickers to the bottom of the wash basket and decided she wouldn't see Marty Lowe again. Yet somehow he became a fixture. He was dependable, loyal, gentle, and she knew he loved her with all his kind heart. Even now he hoped he could persuade her not to leave Hayborough and go to university, but Kara knew she would never change her mind, even though Lou had already changed hers.

She was going steady with Paul, had stopped sharing dreams with Kara about living in London. Louise had a different dream now, of buying a semi-detached house on the Edgeway Estate and following a career in banking.

Kara wanted to be Patti Smith, to write poetry and songs of her own, or to become a famous artist – Frida Kahlo or Paula Rego – and dress in vintage tea dresses and Vivienne Westwood. She bought glossy fashion magazines, imagined shopping in the King's Road, living in a flat in Camden, smoking Sobranie Blues. She wanted to see Istanbul and Paris, to travel on the Trans-Siberian Railway in winter. And she knew all these things would happen, and all the past would be forgotten, when she left Hayborough and High Rigg behind and went to university.

Kara slipped through the yard gate and ran up the steps that led to the lane just as Marty switched off the bike engine. But before she could put on her helmet he unfastened his own and hung it over the handlebars.

'I thought we'd stay in this afternoon,' he said, grinning. He pulled a cassette tape from his pocket. 'I've got that Ramones album.'

'But, Mam . . .'

'Yer mam's gone out, Kara. I saw her on the bus – she waved at me.'

'Well yes, I know, I just meant that she might come back, and . . .' She shrugged and trailed off, knowing it was a waste of time.

Marty led her up the narrow staircase that twisted round twice before it reached the attic. He snapped open the cassette box and slid the new tape into her player, then quickly undressed and climbed into the narrow bed.

'Come on,' he said, smiling. 'Since when have you been so coy? You'll be away for a few days now, and I'm going to miss you.'

Kara stepped out of her jeans and squeezed in at his side. Yet although her body was there with him, her head was already in London, at the Tate and the National Gallery, walking through Leicester Square, window shopping in Carnaby Street.

It was after Marty lit his cigarette, when they were still laid together, her head resting on his chest, that she realised he hadn't used a condom.

'Don't worry about it, Kara – I forgot, that's all. I didn't hear you complain in the heat of the moment. It'll be fine. You know I'd stick by you if you got pregnant, don't you?'

'That's not the point,' she said, jumping up. 'I don't

want a baby, I want a life!'

He looked hurt for a moment, then his face lit up again as he remembered something.

'Pass me my jacket, will you?'

He rummaged through the inside pocket of his leather and pulled out a small jeweller's box. Kara gasped in alarm before she could stop herself, but Marty grinned again, misreading it as a good sign, as a gasp of excitement.

He flicked open the box and held it out to her.

'I know you don't want to get engaged for a while. But I want us to make a commitment to each other, for you to have something as a symbol, as a sign to the world that we're going steady. So I got you this.'

He held out a simple heart-shaped signet ring and reached for her left hand.

'It's a promise ring – just like they give to each other in America. Do you like it?'

Kara looked at him, saw him search her face for the love he was so sure would be there. How could she break his heart? She held out her left hand and allowed him to slip the gold heart onto her ring finger.

After Marty left she took it off and held it in her hand for a moment, feeling the weight of it like a tiny anchor, wondering whether to wear it when she went to London.

She glanced up into her grandfather's eyes, watching her from the photograph in the hallway, somehow raffish even in his RAF uniform. Her gran told her that when he was a child he'd been given a violin which his parents had scrimped and saved for, only for him to swap it at school for a ukulele. His father had never forgiven him, but Kara thought the ukulele sounded much more fun. Her mam said he'd smoked too much, always had a cigarette dangling from the corner of his lips, that his fingers were as brown and stained as the inside of an old teapot. She said he'd died too young, peacefully in his sleep, that Granny Eileen had loved him more than the world and had been sad since the day he died.

Next to him there was a photograph of Gran holding Mam's brother. The baby boy had been christened Eddie Junior, but he'd died before his first birthday. She had hoped to make up for it by having several grandchildren, yet Mam had only wanted Kara.

'Just one girl each, history repeating itself,' Gran always said, with a small, sad laugh.

'My advice to you, young Kara, is to go to university and get yourself a career. Find a man if you must – but pick one who loves you more than you love him or you'll be setting yourself up for heartache, as your old gran knows only too well. And don't waste your time looking for Mr Right, he's as likely to come along as an omnibus to the moon.'

But she'd never been sure about her gran's theory regarding men. It sounded like accepting second best, making do, compromising. Marty fit Gran's profile – he loved Kara more than she loved him, and because of that he could never hurt her. Maybe she was already settling for less, for something she didn't truly want, subconsciously protecting her fragile heart.

Kara slipped the ring onto the middle finger of her right hand and went back up to her room to pack.

All Our Squandered Beauty

THREE

There were ten of them on the London trip, and they were accompanied by their own art teacher, Miss Arnott, and the new tutor, Leo Chapman. He was in his early thirties and had only started at the college that year, having recently moved up to Yorkshire from his native Oxford. The rumour was that he'd separated from his wife. The girls all loved his bohemian good looks, his easy smile, the way he flouted the rules by wearing an old brown leather jacket and jeans.

They arrived in London late on the Monday evening and went straight to their small guest house near Marble Arch. Louise and Kara were to share a cramped room with a draughty communal bathroom at the other end of the corridor, yet Kara was as excited as if they were staying in a five-star hotel on Piccadilly. After a quick supper in a nearby Wimpy they went up to their room and undressed, wrapping themselves in the faded candlewick bedspreads before opening the windows onto the tiny balcony that looked out over Sussex Gardens. They lit cigarettes, blew the smoke extravagantly into the cool evening air. Street lamps bathed them in orange light and traffic thundered up and down the Edgware Road.

'It reminds me of that night in the park,' said Louise. 'The night we thought everything was going to be magical when we discovered London.'

Kara remembered that night vividly. It was the summer holidays of '75: a hot evening at the tail end of August. They were fourteen.

They sat at the top of the playground slide, looking down the hill towards the sea, hearts a little heavy with that end-of-summer feeling. They started to plan their perfect futures, talked of the shine and gloss of distant cities, how they'd work as journalists, share a flat in London somewhere on the expensive side of the Monopoly board, travel around Europe on exciting assignments, and their boyfriends would look like those in the picture stories in *Jackie* magazine.

There was an unusual warmth and softness in the air that night, as though they'd made it somewhere else already – to a place more gentle, where the air was full of fragrant flowers, where boys whispered in Italian and the put-put of scooters could be heard on a distant coastal road.

Then the world fell silent, and in that strange, unnatural quiet there was a second when Kara knew, knew for one brief moment of startling clarity, that life would be good and worth the wait. And when she looked at Lou, Kara could tell she felt it too, and they each held the new knowing close to their ribs, not daring to speak of it in case it wasn't true.

They closed the windows and shut out the noise of the Edgware Road, climbed into bed, already anticipating the next three days: Soho and Bloomsbury, Selfridges and Bond Street, the National and the Tate, Trafalgar Square and Tower Bridge. And first, the following morning, a viewing of an important private collection at the Laing Gallery in Whitechapel, for which Miss Arnott had managed to get them tickets.

Kara was awake at 6 a.m., aware of the thrum of early traffic and the bright stripe of sunlight slicing between the cheap curtains. At 8 a.m. she crept along the threadbare carpet to the bathroom, startled by the hiss and flare of the gas geyser, wary of the loose bolt on the door, the sounds of other guests rattling the handle.

The breakfast room was in the basement, where a faint odour of damp mingled with the smell of cheap bacon and burnt toast. Kara opened a pot of honey and thought of Da. On the mornings Mam had started work early at the library, he'd made toast for her before she set off to school, and he told her the swirls of honey dripping from the spoon were locks of mermaid hair.

After breakfast they walked to Marble Arch to catch the Tube to Aldgate East. The air was warm and gritty, and in between the usual chemists', newsagents' and hardware shops, there were restaurants with elaborate hookah pipes on the tables, shops selling exotic fruit and vegetables and Persian carpets. Kara remembered a house she'd seen in one of her glossy magazines: the light flooding in through a huge bay window filled with macramé planters, white floorboards strewn with rugs just like these, their intricate patterns woven from the finest silk threads. One day she'd have a room just the same.

She loved the bustle of the Tube station, the whoosh of stale air that preceded the arrival of a train, the strange mixture of smells – perfume and sweat, grease and dust, ozone and oil, spent electricity, all wrapped up in something faintly metallic.

At the private gallery, one of the smaller rooms was hung with several abstract paintings of the sea by a young artist called Hazel Mavering. Kara sat on the bench in the centre and stared at each of them in turn. She'd never seen the sea depicted like this before. In the pictures they studied with Miss Arnott, the sea was Turner's washes of ocean and sky, Atkinson Grimshaw's moonlight on still water. Or they were paintings of shipwrecks: anxious women waiting on the shore, waves crashing on rocks beneath brooding skies, or tall ships, full sail on steady seas.

Yet in Hazel Mavering's paintings there was no sky or coastline, no ships, no rocks – you were in the sea, beneath the sea, fighting against the current, drowning, surfing, giving yourself up to the waves. There was only the water. The paintings were arguments with the sea, walls of spume and spray, haunting, wild, savage and brutal, exactly the way she saw the sea herself. They exploded with energy, beautiful yet terrifying. They were every shade of blue, green and grey, flecked with white, stirred with yellow and ochre; they were the sand whipped up in the water, the sunlight seen through waves. They were foreboding and joyous, paintings of life and death, of limitless distances, rolling, curving, crashing.

And they took Kara back again to the year after Da's accident, to the March morning she endlessly recalled, the one she'd re-lived on the fishing pier only three days ago.

Mam had set off early for work, leaving Kara's breakfast laid out on the table. She found a letter tucked under the newspaper from a solicitor, confirming the cottage had been sold to a Mr Messruther, and a quotation from a removal firm for moving their things to Granny Eileen's house. She could feel the weight of it in her stomach, the solid certainty, a catch in her throat as the tears welled up.

She couldn't go; she wouldn't leave Da.

Kara put the letters back where she'd found them and carried her pots over to the sink. From the kitchen window she could see the harbour bandaged in early morning mist, the soft grey swell of the sea. Suddenly she knew that today was the day. She wasn't going to school. This would be the day she'd find Da.

She went back upstairs and pulled on her favourite swimming costume, her jeans and red cardigan, then left the cottage and crossed the road to the coble landing. She took nothing with her, not even a towel. She walked down the slipway to the sand, along the shoreline towards the pier. There was hardly anyone around. The day was drab and dull, scudding clouds threatening squally rain. She saw George in the distance, her father's friend, starting up the old tractor to drag his dinghy off the beach. She waved, but he didn't see her.

She slipped off her clothes, left them folded neatly on the sand, her house key tucked inside her cardigan. Then she waded out to Jackson's Rock, to where the seabed fell away and the water darkened. At first the cold was knife-sharp, but the deeper she went the less she could feel it. She remembered hearing a dog bark on the pier as the rushing tide sucked and hissed, churning the sand, threatening to topple her before she reached the rock, each wave choking off her breath. Yet when the moment came, she didn't resist. She smiled as she disappeared beneath the water, because the tide would take her to Da, to the other side of the sea, and she was ready to go.

And there in the Laing Gallery she gave herself up to the sea once again, and for those few minutes she was totally immersed, her breath jagged as she felt the water close over her head.

She jumped when Leo Chapman sat down beside her.

'I take it you like these pictures, Kara?'

She nodded, but couldn't trust herself to answer, raw emotion knotting in her throat. She was aware of Leo's arm pressed against hers, the soft wool of his jumper tickling her skin, the sandalwood scent of his cologne and the faint smell of spearmint on his breath.

Kara looked down at her tightly clasped hands and waited for the threat of tears to subside.

'I love them,' she said, eventually. 'I've never seen anything like them before, nothing that captures the sea like this, as though the artist was inside a storm, drowning.'

He touched the back of her hand with his index finger.

'If I ever win the football pools I'll buy you one,' he said. 'Come on, let's catch up with the others.'

Leo stayed close to Kara wherever they went. He stood with her on the Tube, sat next to her on the bus, made sure he was on the same table when they stopped for lunch. Yet he did it so casually she was never sure whether it was simply coincidence.

They stopped to make sketches of everything they saw, and he was always at her elbow, advising her on perspective, praising her work, noting how quickly and deftly she caught the essence of a scene, the character in a face, the light, the energy.

In the pub he stood with Kara and Louise in a smoky corner, supplying them with cigarettes and pints of cider, ignoring Miss Arnott, who kept reminding him that they were only just seventeen. They stood together, clutching their drinks, hip bones bumping as the crowd jostled around them. Kara watched Leo closely, drank in every molecule of him, took in the shape of his hands, the line of pale hairs that ran up his tanned forearm, the green of his eyes, the vertical crease that appeared between them when he talked about something serious, the distracted way he ran his fingers through his hair.

When Kara and Louise were alone in their hotel room, Kara wanted to talk about him, to re-live every moment of the evening, every glance, every accidental brush of the arm. But Louise fell asleep straight away, and Kara went out onto the balcony, listening to the drone of taxis and night buses as she gazed up at the sodium sky.

She'd fallen in love with London, just as she'd expected. She was excited by the limitless possibilities the city promised, had sketched the pulse and clamour of the thronging streets, the glitter and shine of window displays, the skyline from Hampstead Heath. She'd cooled her feet in the fountains in Trafalgar Square, watched men in shiny suits pull in gullible punters for Soho peepshows, marvelled at the mysteries of sound waves as she pressed her lips to the walls of the

Whispering Gallery in St Paul's, was enthralled by the magic of the dark, starry galaxies in the planetarium at Madame Tussauds. Yet although a thousand images crowded her mind, she couldn't stop thinking about Hazel Mavering's sea paintings.

On their last evening they went back to Leicester Square, to the Angus Steak House, and Leo slid into the booth at Kara's side, his knee brushing against hers. They drank red wine that went straight to her head, and both Leo and Miss Arnott praised her work, said she'd come on in leaps and bounds, asked her if she'd ever thought of taking her art further. Outside, in the stillness of the warm evening, lights shone out from every bar, restaurant and cinema, and a couple sat together on the bench across from the steak house, the girl resting her head against the boy's shoulder.

At that moment, it felt to Kara as though this could be the real world – this could be her world. It was no longer a fantasy; it was as if life was finally beginning. Kara wanted to be living and breathing this city every day: studying poetry in the British Library, walking along the Embankment with new friends, going to parties and galleries, poetry readings and French films. She knew that in London everything would be different.

When they got on the train to come home, Leo sat with Miss Arnott and hardly spoke to Kara. But as they arrived at Hayborough he helped them all to lift their bags down from the luggage rack. As he handed Kara her rucksack he slipped a slim, flat package into the open pocket on the front, smiled as he touched his finger to his lips. She opened it as soon as she got home. It was a small print, just six inches by eight, of a painting by Hazel Mavering. A single wave, tumbling, the darkest blue, deepest grey, flecked through with ochre and grey and white, spume flying and scattering like so many diamonds.

FOUR

Kara arrived early at college the next morning and hung around the art room in the hope of seeing Leo. But he didn't appear until after the first bell had rung, so all she saw was a glimpse of him down the corridor as she rushed off to her tutor group.

In fact she hardly saw him at all over the following week as he was invigilating final exams, and when she did catch sight of him across the canteen she was certain he'd seen her, yet he quickly looked away. Kara convinced herself she was being paranoid, but something stopped her from talking about it to Louise. She hadn't even mentioned the Mavering print, and when Louise came over to the farmhouse she slipped it into her dressing table drawer.

The following Tuesday afternoon she finally caught Leo alone in the art room. She stood in the doorway for a minute and watched him. He had his back to her, concentrating on rearranging a pile of sketches. Before she'd had chance to think about what she was doing, she slipped inside and closed the door, sliding the latch across.

'Kara! I was going to put a message in your pigeonhole this week.'

'I thought you were ignoring me,' she said.

'Of course not, I've just been busy. But it's better if we're not caught inside a locked room! You're not even in my tutor group, and . . . '

'Don't panic,' Kara said, laughing. 'Why are you so nervous about talking to students? Has something happened?'

Leo shook his head, yet he still looked worried. 'It's . . . well you know what gossip is like.'

He walked across the room and slid the bolt back, pulling the door open again.

'I've been thinking about you though, Kara. I think your art shows great promise, and Miss Arnott agrees. I know you're set on doing English Lit at university, but I thought I might persuade you to take time out this summer on an art placement? It's a funded place for a gifted student, and I thought of you. It's a chance to travel to Europe – to Greece to be precise – to work with some other talented artists. It would be a great opportunity to paint the sea – your favourite subject. What do you think?'

'On my own?'

'Of course not – I'd be going with you. I tutor some of the classes. The foundation is run by an old friend of mine, Philipe Patou.'

'And where would I stay?'

'We all stay together in the villa, a rambling place on the hillside above a beautiful beach.'

Kara's heart jumped. Was he asking what she thought he was asking? Or was it just what he said – an art placement? She looked at him, wanting to see the intention in his eyes without having to ask, needing it to be an unspoken thing between them. He smiled and met her gaze; she saw everything she needed to see.

'I'd love to go! But I need to ask my mother, and what about the details . . . when, for how long, would we fly?'

He laughed at her breathlessness, her excitement, her words tumbling over themselves.

'Of course we'll fly! And of course you need to ask your mother! I'll write to her formally, and I can go down to the library one day after classes to talk to her. To both of you, if you'd like?'

Kara was relieved that Leo had suggested the library as a meeting place. She wouldn't have wanted him to come up to the farm, to sit in the flagged kitchen with the damp patch above the window, with Gran's porcelain shepherdesses cluttering the shelves, the old fringed chenille cloth still covering the table beneath the checked one, the moth-eaten stuffed otter in the parlour, the faded family photos on the hallway walls. Neither she nor Mam ever noticed the jumble and mess; it comforted them to leave it as it was, full of the precious memories of both their childhoods.

Mam had taken her to Granny Eileen's for Sunday tea every other week when she was a child. It had always been the same food: salmon paste sandwiches made with doorstop slices, then chocolate Swiss roll and a trifle to follow. Every week they sat up at the table and used the best china, the fringing tickling Kara's knees. And as she ate her trifle she would already be anticipating the quarter of aniseed balls that Mam would buy her from Mrs Bevitt's sweet shop in Hayborough before they caught the bus back to Elmwick.

When they'd lived in the village, most of Kara's school friends had mothers who stayed at home or worked in the herring sheds, but Mam had always worked at the library in Hayborough, and this kept her apart from the other women in Elmwick. The fishermen's wives and widows helped out with the nets, met up in the village hall on Thursdays to knit sweaters for their men and gossip over tea and cake. When they saw Mam walking to the bus stop in her work suit and smart shoes, they might nod in acknowledgement, but they didn't speak to her. Kara always knew her mother wasn't like them, had sometimes wished she was, had understood even as a child that it was easier to fit in than walk your own path.

Mam was tall and elegant, long and graceful like a wading bird, her hair was red like Granny Eileen's, her eyes were the deepest blue. She was the opposite of Da. He'd been dark-haired, compact and wiry, his movements deft. His eyes altered colour as swiftly as a chameleon's skin. They couldn't be labelled as light brown, yet neither were they hazel or milk chocolate or caramel; they were all of these things at different times of day in the changing light. Kara had inherited Da's dark glossy hair, yet she was tall like Mam, and her eyes were the palest hazel.

Mam was beautiful, yet she hated her photograph taken. She would slip on sunglasses to hide her face, or hold up a hand to shield her eyes, squinting at the camera, complaining of having been asked to look straight into the light.

Kara knew her mother had always wanted to get away from the farm, had dreamed of becoming a writer or a journalist. She'd gone to the grammar school in Hayborough, just as Kara had, and she'd been set to go to university.

'But then she met me and all else was forgotten,' Da used to tease. 'She turned my head when I saw her at the farmers' dance that night, and I wasn't going to let her slip through my fingers.'

Whenever he said that, Kara smiled, yet deep inside she felt sad, because she sensed that all else had not been forgotten, that a piece of her mother would always be held back, that she was a little distant from everyone, that she walked alone through the world.

Her mam was won over by Leo Chapman – his easy charm, his wide smile. She thought the art placement was a great opportunity and she agreed to it after very little persuasion. They would be going at the start of the holidays in just over two weeks' time, and they would be there for three weeks, staying on the tiny island of Lyros.

'All Kara needs is a little spending money, Mrs Bradshaw. Food and board is taken care of – and the flight. Art materials will be provided. The foundation will even pay to fast-track Kara's passport.'

'There's no need for that, we can get a one-year passport from the post office,' her mam replied. Kara said nothing to contradict her, yet she had wanted the ten-year one, positive this would be the first of many foreign adventures.

After Leo left, Kara was too impatient to hang around in the library waiting for her mother to finish work. She wanted to go down to Louise's house and tell her about the trip. As she walked along the main street she felt light-headed and dizzy, scared and giddy. There was so much to think about – the excitement of flying and visiting Greece, the chance to paint, precious time alone with Leo.

It was when she stopped to cross the road at the corner that she noticed the woman walking ahead of her towards the bus station. Tall and lithe, strong shoulders, thick blonde hair swinging down her back. The way she walked, carried herself, it had to be her. It was Lola Armitage.

Kara dashed across the road, keeping her distance. She wanted to go up to her, grab her arm, ask her what she was doing here, question her about Da. But she hung back, unable to approach her, scared to ask questions when she was frightened of the answers.

Lola hadn't seen her; she headed down to the end of the bus stands and jumped straight on the 288 for Elmwick. Kara's heart flipped. She followed her onto the bus and sat down quickly at the front in the hope she wouldn't be noticed.

When they pulled up at Elmwick harbour, Kara looked out of the window to hide her face. After everyone else got off, she slipped out quickly behind them and followed Lola along the foreshore road. She went into one of the cottages at the south end, the row where she'd lived seven years ago, yet Kara wasn't sure it was the same house as before. As the door closed behind her, she wondered what to do. Should she knock, feign surprise at seeing her and pretend she'd been looking for someone else? Should she come back another day? What if there was someone else living there with her? What if . . .? No, that was ridiculous, she couldn't allow herself to think that, not even for a moment.

FIVE

Kara sat on the beach wall in the warm afternoon sun, wondering whether to leave, trying to gather the courage to stay. Just as she saw the bus turning at the end of the road, Lola came out of the house. Although she was a distance away, Kara could see she was wearing a beach wrap and had a towel folded over her arm. She walked quickly down to the water's edge, and Kara's heart banged and fluttered against her ribs like a frightened bird. She held her breath as Lola untied the wrap and dropped her things onto the sand. She watched her stride down to the water and wade out, still slender and muscular in her costume, admired the strong, graceful strokes she remembered so well. She swam twice across the bay, sleek as a seal. Kara shielded her eyes from the sun with her hand, watched Lola step out of the sea just as she'd done the first time she saw her.

Kara was eight when she asked Da to teach her to swim. He bought her a pair of inflatable water wings and taught her in the shallows, promising that if she ate all her cabbage then she'd be strong enough to swim without her wings the year after. In the summer that followed she'd gone from strength to strength, but Da never let her out of his sight or swim far out. He understood Elmwick's currents, how quickly the tide could turn, how easy it was to drown even when the water appeared calm.

That third summer, July had been dry yet cool. Despite the blue skies and still seas, the sand felt cold between Kara's toes, and the water wasn't often warm enough for swimming. She still went down to the beach with Da in the late afternoons. There'd been some old nets washed up on recent tides, and he was checking to see if there was anything worth salvaging.

One afternoon, when the tide was at low ebb, they saw a man in the distance talking to a woman who'd just come out of the sea. Kara had been watching her through the binoculars, trying to learn from her sure, fast strokes. The woman picked up her towel and wrapped it around her, hugging it to her chest. Their voices carried up the beach, the man's getting louder, the woman's sounding anxious.

She tried to walk away, but the man followed her, and Da strode quickly down the beach towards them. When the man saw him approaching, he walked off in the opposite direction. Da picked up the woman's things and they strolled slowly back up the sand towards Kara, laughing and joking then, as though nothing had happened. The woman was tall and slim, yet muscular, her blonde hair turned dark by the sea. She wore a bright red swimming costume with stripes down the side, the type that professional swimmers wore, not like Mam's flimsy bikinis. As she came closer, Kara could see that the woman was Lola Armitage, the sculptor who everyone was talking about. She was renting a house for the summer at the far end of the village, and could often be seen riding around on a rusty bicycle with a basket filled with sketchbooks and modelling clay. She dressed in floaty cotton dresses and painters' smocks, tied her hair up with long silk scarves, smoked exotic cigarettes in an ebony holder, drank pints of bitter in the Crown & Anchor with the fishermen. None of their wives approved. They said she was 'fast'.

Kara had been curious about her – she was so different to everyone else in the village – but now, although she couldn't have explained why, she didn't want Lola to talk to her da. There was something in the way she looked at him, the way she rested her fingers lightly on his wrist, the way she tipped her head to one side and smiled, that made Kara feel jealous. It was as though Lola was sharing something with Da that Kara didn't understand, something beyond her knowledge, something that gave her power. She couldn't have explained it to anyone, but she was suddenly filled with doubt. Her father wasn't hers alone as she'd always thought, and everything she'd believed to be secure seemed as flimsy as paper. For the first time she understood that Da could be taken from her, knew it would be impossible to stop it happening.

Behind them, Nelson the cat sat on the sea wall and looked at them with his one wide orange eye. Lola laughed and pointed.

'I see that cat watching me every day,' she said. 'He spooks me.'

'Kara can tell you the story of Nelson, can't you, pet?'

She shook her head and pretended to be untangling the pile of nets on the sand. Da ruffled her hair and smiled.

'Nelson is a ship's cat who was drowned at sea,' he said. 'He was returned to shore by the power of magic.

If you find two pieces of matching sea glass in the shape of cats' eyes, and sleep with them under your pillow, then a lost cat will be re-born and live forever.'

Kara felt herself blushing. She clenched her fists tightly and looked away from them both. How could he betray her by telling Lola their special story? That story was theirs and theirs alone. And now Da had spoiled it and Lola would laugh at them.

Lola smiled, the type of smile that grown-ups gave you when they thought you were stupid. She picked up her things from where Da had put them down on the dry sand and turned to go.

'Thanks again for getting rid of that creep,' she called over her shoulder. 'And just so you know, the cat's name isn't Nelson, it's Jaffa, and I was told he lost his eye in a fight with Billy Norton's terrier.'

They watched Lola walk up the slipway and climb astride her bicycle, saw her pedal slowly along the road. When she was out of sight, Kara turned for home without saying a word to Da, aware that something had changed, an imperceptible shift she didn't understand. And for the first time she felt a sense of the enormity of the world and her powerlessness within it.

Lola was walking up the beach towards her now, and Kara felt the same sense of loss, the same uncertainty, the same weight of stones in her mouth as she had all those years ago.

As she got closer, the woman narrowed her eyes against the bright glare of the sand.

'Are you okay?' she asked.

Kara realised she had been standing motionless,

staring, for several minutes. She took in the woman's face, the pale blue eyes, the full bottom lip, the scattering of freckles across her upturned nose. It wasn't Lola.

'No, er, yes . . . I er . . . I thought you were someone I knew . . .'

The woman smiled. 'I'm guessing it's someone you don't care too much for.'

Kara laughed, embarrassed to have betrayed her feelings so easily. She shook her head and the woman continued up the beach.

She waited until she saw her go inside her cottage, then walked across to the bus stop to check the time of the next bus back to Hayborough. All her excitement about Leo and the art trip had faded now; all she could think about was Lola, the way she'd looked at Da, the way she'd dismissed Kara as nothing more than a silly child who was in the way of what she wanted. The trip to Greece seemed unreal, like something she didn't deserve, something that was part of someone else's life. And when she reached the bus stop she discovered there wasn't a bus for another hour.

Kara headed back to the beach, walked down towards the sea, strolled along the shoreline, her head bowed as she searched the sand for sea glass and shells, trying to still her mind. She picked up a handful of small flat stones and threw them one by one into the sea, skimming them as Da had taught her. A larger pebble stood out among the dull grey: the size of an old half-crown, dotted with ochre and pink.

She remembered the stone she found on her seventh birthday, smooth and flat and perfectly round, as though rolled out by a fairy's rolling pin. Stippled with blue and grey and pink, freckled like an egg. She slipped it into her pocket without showing it to Da, carried it home to give to him later.

Yet when she took it out to show Mam, it was dry and dull, the colours faded and muted. Before she handed it to Da, she held it under the tap to show him how beautiful it was when it shone. He took it from her and smiled.

'That can be fixed, my lovely sea sprite. We must leave it outside in the garden when it's a full moon. Then the elves will polish your stone until it shines.'

Kara waited impatiently for the next eight days to pass before the full moon, then placed the stone at the edge of the flower border before she went to bed.

'Are you sure the elves will find it here?' she asked Da.

'Don't worry, Kara, they'll see it.'

When she went into the garden the following morning she hardly dared hope to find the stone altered. Yet there it was at the edge of the flowers, shining, smooth, the blues and the pinks as bright as before.

'I want you to have it, Da,' she said, holding it out to him. 'You must take it with you wherever you go – for luck.'

He closed his hand around the stone and pressed it to his chest.

'I'll never let it out of my sight, Kara. I'll hold onto it as tightly as the barnacles grip Canny Lass's hull.'

It was years before she realised that Da had varnished the stone after she'd gone to bed, and when she found out she made sure he never knew.

When she turned back at the end of the beach she saw someone waving from the road. He ran down the slipway, a crash helmet in his hand, walked towards her across the sand. As he got closer she realised it was Jake Andrews, the lad from Ravengrove who'd talked to her on the fish pier.

'Hi Kara, I thought it was you! What are you doing over in Elmwick?'

'Nothing much,' she said. 'I used to live here when I was a kid. I like to come back now and again to walk on the beach or swim. It's quieter than Hayborough – no tourists around.'

He nodded, yet something in his eyes suggested he knew she wasn't telling the whole truth. Kara remembered what Louise had told her about his brother.

'I'm sorry about your brother,' she said impulsively.

He nodded again. 'Aye, it was a bad do, losing him . . .' He gestured towards the road. 'Do you want a lift back to Hayborough? I'm going across there now and I could drop you at the bus station if you like. It'll be another half hour before the next bus from here.'

They walked up the slipway together. She took the helmet he handed her from the top box and climbed up behind him. His neck was long and lean, and when the wind whipped away the dark curls of his hair, she could see the smooth pale skin above his jacket collar. It was such a small thing, yet it made him seem achingly vulnerable, and she wanted to wrap her arms around him.

When she arrived back at the farm it was already dusk,

and Marty's bike was parked on the lane. Her heart sank. She knew she'd have to tell him about the art trip – if Mam hadn't told him already.

He was sitting with her mother at the kitchen table, and although they both smiled she could feel the tension in the room. She guessed that Marty already knew about Greece.

'Where have you been?' he asked with false brightness. 'You knew I was coming up this evening.'

'Sorry, Marty, I went down to Louise's. Time just ran away with us. Shall we go straight out?'

Kara went into the hall, fetched her leather jacket and helmet, ignoring Mam as she fussed about her not eating her tea.

'I'll get something at Charelli's,' she called out as she shut the door.

She wanted to go somewhere crowded, where Marty couldn't nag her about the art trip.

But when they pulled up outside the cafe she saw that Paul's bike was there, and she couldn't risk seeing Louise right now when she'd lied about going over to her house.

'Let's not go in,' she said. 'I don't feel like talking to other people. Shall we drive up to the forest instead?'

She really didn't want to be alone with him, but she had no choice.

It was another warm evening and the darkness was soft as velvet. Marty drove through the woods to the highest point, where you could sit on the ridge of the hill and look out across a valley of trees towards the rolling heather. It seemed so still and quiet here at the edge of the moorland, yet twigs cracked beneath invisible paws and owls swooped on soundless wings across the valley floor.

They spread out their jackets and lay down together on the warm bed of pine needles, bright stars shining between the tall spruce trees.

Kara waited for Marty to speak, but when he did it wasn't about the art trip.

'Do you think you're pregnant?' he asked.

His voice was hopeful, not wary or anxious. She realised that he wanted her to say yes. Because then the art trip wouldn't matter, then she'd be his, bound to him, tied into the future he wanted. His apprenticeship at the garage was almost complete, he'd just taken his last exams, and he'd told her many times that when he was on full wage as a qualified mechanic they could get married. Kara had never taken him seriously, always knowing that she'd be leaving Hayborough and Marty behind, yet now she realised the mistake she'd made leading him on.

'You forgot the condoms on purpose that time, didn't you?'

He turned towards her and propped himself up on his elbow. Even though the woods were dark, she could see he was smiling.

'I just want us to be a family,' he said. 'I love you, Kara. You are pregnant, aren't you? I know it.'

'No, Marty, I don't think I'm pregnant. But I am hungry. Let's go back down to Charelli's.'

She stood up and shrugged on her jacket, hoping against hope that her words would prove to be true.

SIX

The week before she flew to Greece, Kara went shopping in Hayborough with her mother. They bought her a beautiful cheesecloth dress and a bikini from Chelsea Girl, and on the morning she was setting off, Mam came into her bedroom holding out a pair of gold hoop earrings.

'Here, you can borrow these, pet. They'll look lovely with that dress. I want you to have a good time, but be careful, won't you?'

'Careful of what?' she laughed. 'I'm going to be fine.'

As she closed her wardrobe door she saw Da's gloves. She pulled them out and pressed them to her face, inhaled the faint scent of leather, almost sure she could still detect the wood and citrus of his cologne, yet she knew that could only be conjured from memory now. She'd snatched the gloves from the hall drawer the week after his accident, had pressed them to her face, inhaled the smell of dust and sea and sweat before slipping them onto her own small hands. She had sobbed until there were no more tears, remembering the feel of Da's strong fingers intertwined with hers, their autumn walks on the cliffs. Yet after that day she couldn't bear to touch the gloves again; even the thought of seeing them was unbearable. She left them under her pillow, out of sight, and when her mam changed the bed sheets she always put them back exactly as she'd found them.

When Kara finally had the courage to take them out again, the scent was already much fainter, and she cried for the time she'd wasted. The last traces of Da were disappearing, and she was scared that soon she wouldn't be able to remember his voice or his face.

Kara heard Leo's taxi on the lane and tried to rush out, to say goodbye at the doorway, bashing her case against the gate in her rush, but her mother ran up the steps after her and was leaning into the open car window before she'd even climbed in at the other side.

'Look after her won't you, Leo?'

'Of course, Evie, don't worry about a thing. This is going to be a marvellous experience for Kara.'

When they stepped off the plane they were enveloped in a cloud of warm air filled with the scent of herbs and pine resin, of flowers and hot tarmac. Dusty bougainvillea flowered around the runway and inside the terminal building overhead fans turned lazily above the luggage carousel.

The so-called ferry was nothing more than a small boat with an outboard motor and a canvas cover to keep off the sun. As Kara handed her case across the narrow gangplank she felt a prick of apprehension, yet when she looked out past the harbour at the calm, clear water, the tiny island of Lyros already visible across the bay, she pushed the fear firmly down.

The taxi bumped along the narrow streets of the port town and then took the coast road through the silver-green olive groves that pulsed with the sound of cicadas. Kara caught glimpses of turquoise coves as the road wound left and right, then they climbed a steep hill and the villa was there ahead of them. It was an old, rambling house, newly whitewashed with a terracotta roof, and behind the closed green shutters the interior was cool.

They were greeted by Leo's friend, Philipe. He was tall and loose-limbed, dressed in a crumpled linen suit. He had an air of effortless style, of easy money. He was a good-looking man, but his eyes were a cold grey, and Kara could see that his face was a little puffy from drink. At his side was a tall woman with thick auburn curls, wearing a long patterned kaftan, who kissed her on both cheeks and introduced herself as Marion.

'So young, and soooo beautiful!' she exclaimed, stroking Kara's cheek. She took her by the arm and showed her to two bedrooms at the back of the villa.

'I've put you in separate rooms, as I wasn't quite sure?' she said quietly.

Kara blushed. How could Marion have guessed about her and Leo? It wasn't as though there was anything to know – she wasn't even sure about it herself yet.

The room was simply furnished, the window covered with a curtain of thick handmade lace, and when she held it to one side she was looking out onto a small walled garden filled with lemon and olive trees, pots of bright geraniums.

She unpacked her clothes and arranged her toiletries in the bathroom. It was only when she took out her box of tampons that she thought about the date, tried to count backwards to her last period. It was the week before the London trip, just before the afternoon when Marty 'forgot' the condom – which meant she was already two weeks late. But this wasn't the first time she'd been late. Her periods were often irregular, and she'd been more than an entire month late before now.

She looked at her new dress laid out on the bed, Mam's gold hoop earrings, her Indian sandals, and she knew she wasn't going to let anything spoil these precious three weeks. She changed into the dress, tied her hair up with a patterned silk scarf, then went back out to the front terrace, where Marion had told her they met for drinks before dinner. When she passed Leo's room the door was ajar. She saw that he had a large double bed and full-length windows that opened out into the same private garden.

'Here she is!' said Marion. 'In her fabulous dress. Boys, look how gorgeous she is. Come and sit by me, Kara, and tell me all about yourself.'

She patted the chair next to her and poured Kara a tall glass of cloudy liquid from a large jug.

'Ouzo and water,' she said. 'Aniseed! Delicious!'

Kara sipped it tentatively. It was cold and refreshing, and she drank the rest far too quickly. The second glass made her head buzz. Leo and Philipe were deep in conversation and she leaned across the table to take one of Leo's cigarettes.

'Have one of these,' said Marion, offering a pack of St Moritz. Kara pulled out the long cigarette with its gold band and picked up Marion's Dunhill lighter from the table. As she inhaled, the menthol flavour surprised her and she almost coughed. She reached for her drink and took a long swig, then took the pack of St Moritz and turned the turquoise and gold box around in her hand. Everyone looked so beautiful in the evening light, so exotic, as though they'd stepped straight from the pages of one of her expensive fashion magazines. Kara knew this was where she wanted to be right now, yet at the same time she could see there was something flat and two-dimensional about it, something a little unreal. There was no shadow or depth.

Across the water, the lights on the mainland winked in the gathering dusk. She watched car headlights as they wound down the hillside, imagined Greek families laughing over their dinner in quayside restaurants, red-checked tablecloths and wild flowers on the tables.

'So when do the others arrive?' she asked.

She saw Leo glance up, but he didn't reply.

'The others?' asked Marion. 'Well Lara and Monty did say they'd drive down from Yugoslavia sometime this summer – they're in Dubrovnik as we speak – but I'm not sure they'll get over here while you're still with us.'

She leaned across and patted Kara's knee.

'No, it's just the four of us for now. And we're going to have such wonderful fun, aren't we, darling?'

She turned to Philipe as she spoke. He nodded and smiled.

'Of course we are. We're going to show you a good time, Kara.'

'And what about the art classes?'

Marion looked confused.

'Classes? Well you and Leo will go out painting together I expect – we never see him in the mornings, do we, Philipe?'

When she saw Leo's face, she realised the

misunderstanding and laughed.

'Oh Kara! Those "other" art students are just a convenient invention of Leo's! How else would he get your mother to agree to let you come out here? I hope you're not shocked? Leo, why didn't you tell the girl before you actually got here? You are incorrigible!'

She stood up and walked towards the villa.

'I'll tell Katerina to bring us some wine and nibbles. Dinner will be another hour I think.'

Kara was embarrassed. Ashamed of her own stupidity, her naivety, her gullibility. Yet Miss Arnott had been taken in too – and her mother. She knew she was a hypocrite, because it wasn't that she minded Leo lying to them – she would have gone along with his ruse and come to Greece anyway. She only minded that Leo had deceived *her*. If he had deceived her about that, what else would he lie about?

Yet the chatter went on around the table as though there was nothing to consider, nothing to discuss, as though it were a triviality.

Kara ate her dinner, drank too much wine, went to bed early saying she was tired. Yet she knew she wouldn't sleep, that she would wait, half scared, yet half hoping that Leo would come to her room. She lay awake, confused and hot, listening to the sounds from the other side of the villa: to Marion's laugh, a loud splash in the swimming pool, Philipe's voice, doors banging. When everything fell silent she got up and went to the window, watched a skinny cat run across the garden, carrying some small grey creature in its mouth. She leaned out and saw that the doors to Leo's room were still open. She could smell cigarette smoke, yet there wasn't a sound from inside. She mouthed his name, yet something stopped her from saying it out loud. Kara knew he wouldn't come; he would be waiting for her to go to him. She pulled the windows closed and climbed back into bed.

SEVEN

There was a private path that led down from the villa to a cove, a winding donkey track thick with fallen olive leaves and cypress needles. The following morning, while the rest of the house was still sleeping, Kara wound her way down the hillside, carrying her sketchbook and pencils.

As she descended the path, she crossed lines of ants, saw lizards dart in and out of cracks, glimpsed the split-second flick of their tongues, watched small beetles pushing balls of leaf mould, and rhino beetles, ink-black, fat as thumbs, hovering like helicopters.

At the bottom of the track there was a flight of uneven steps that took her right down to the cove. It was a narrow shingle beach with the clearest water Kara had ever seen. Shoals of tiny fish, almost translucent, weaved as one in the shallows between fronds of delicate seaweed, and freckled sea cucumbers bobbed in and out on the gentle waves.

She wished she could share it with Da. There were days when the loss of him still hurt too much, when she wanted to stop missing him more than anything else. Yet it was also her biggest fear that days would come and go without her thinking of him once. Here in the cove, she felt close to him, remembering their early mornings on the beach; those special days when her mam started work early and it was just the two of them.

As soon as Kara had heard her mother's alarm clock

through the wall, she'd wrapped herself in a blanket and curled up on the bedroom window seat, knees drawn up to her chin. She listened to the sounds of wheezing floorboards and clanky plumbing, watched the sky for that precious hour when the brightest stars were still faintly visible in the dawn light.

After Mam set off to work, Da always made them a pot of strong tea and his special mermaid toast. Before they left for school he'd crouch down to tie her boots, even though she'd been able to lace them herself since she was four years old. Then they'd head down to the shoreline to search for sea treasure, the flotsam of the night's tide laid out for the taking. Her father collected driftwood for the stove: twisted branches that had travelled across oceans, planks from shipwrecks with their paint peeling back in layers, lengths of faded rope that he could re-use for his nets. But Kara sought out the smooth pebbles, speckled like eggs, and the things the sea had taken from the land and sculpted into gems. Those rounded fragments of broken pottery, dappled with faded patterns of flowers and birds, which she imagined were once delicate teacups, crashing from galley shelves in the wildest of storms, and shards of glass rumbled into opaque nuggets of turquoise, emerald, cornelian and opal.

Da had another name for sea glass; he told Kara she was collecting sailors' souls. He explained that every bead of glass contained the soul of someone lost at sea – a fisherman or sailor or rigger – and each piece took on the colour of the sailor's eyes. It was said a glass soul washing up on the strand was a sign the spirit wished to return to shore as flesh and blood, but this could only come about if they were found by someone who had loved them.

And after the accident Kara still scoured the sand for treasure, yet she only picked out the nuggets of brown and ochre glass, occasionally tricked by the shine of a scrap of seaweed. She thought of Da's eyes as having been the colour of amber, flecked with marmalade and sunshine. There was never any glass to match the colour she remembered, yet still she held each piece in her palm, closing her eyes until she could feel his calloused hand in hers. But the glass always remained cold. She threw it all back into the sea, hurling it as far and as hard as she could, as though to discourage each piece from washing ashore again and condemning her to repeat the same disappointment. She realised that Da couldn't be found on the shore; she would have to swim out to sea if she wanted to find him.

Yet in Lyros she found herself searching for sea glass again in the cove, hoping that Da had somehow made it to the Ionian Sea, where the water was kinder and quieter. The water glittered and lapped the shingle, was permanently blue. It appeared to want to stop awhile, to wash gently to and fro, to take nothing, to give up nothing. The North Sea was always grey and murky, churning sand, sucking at the shore, taking away whatever it wanted, eroding and re-shaping, and only giving up the things it had no more use for. In Greece, the natural world was coming alive again for Kara, she felt closer to nature, to the sea, than she had since Da died, and she knew he was there in the shimmer of the water, in the warmth of the sun on the back of her neck.

She found a piece of amber glass that was as near to the colour of Da's eyes as any she'd ever found before. She zipped it inside her purse to take home, to carry there always amongst her coins, even though she no longer truly believed Da's myths.

There was a tiny uninhabited island to the south that looked as though it would be easy to reach, yet Philipe had warned her about the unsafe currents farther out. Kara felt no fear of swimming to the island from this calm, still cove, yet she knew it would be stupid to ignore the warning. She sat down on a flat rock at the end of the bay with her sketch pad, hoping to capture the beauty of the morning, the sparkle on the sea. But however hard she tried she couldn't grasp the essence of it. The sea was already in her head, in her heart, anchored at her very core, yet it seemed it couldn't be recreated on paper or canvas, or even in words. Something always disappeared, was lost, between her memories, the images in her head, and the paper. So instead of the water she sketched the shells and wildflowers, the beetles and butterflies.

When she returned to the villa the others were only just up, sitting on the terrace with pots of Katerina's dark, gritty coffee, a jar of local honey, a basket of fresh, crusty bread. Swallowtail butterflies and swifts fluttered and swooped above the swimming pool, and Kara crouched down to scoop tiny iridescent insects from the water and watch them rest in the sun until their wings dried.

'What are you doing, Kara?' asked Marion impatiently. 'They're just insects that were stupid enough to fly into the pool. Let them drown! Survival of the fittest and all that.'

Kara looked up at Marion and wondered if she could survive here herself. She had come to paint, to be with Leo, yet somehow it wasn't how she'd imagined it would be and she wasn't sure why.

In the afternoon, Philipe drove them all into town, and they explored the cool darkness of a tiny church, a hundred candles flickering for the souls of lost family. Kara took a long taper and lit her own, dropping a few coins into the metal box. She sat down for a moment in front of the altar, inhaling the heady scent of incense and flowers, listening to the priest praying in his low melodic voice. A woman next to her was leant forward in prayer, muttering her responses to the priest, wooden prayer beads wrapped around her clasped hands. When Kara got up to leave, the woman nodded to her and followed her out of the pew.

Kara stepped back outside into the sunlight, the woman walking behind her, re-tying a dark scarf around her head. She handed Kara a single pink flower and made the sign of the cross, mumbling in Greek. Then she held onto Kara's wrist for a moment and looked back at the church entrance, where Leo and Philipe had just appeared.

'Be careful,' she said in English. 'Beautiful girls must always be careful.'

Before she could answer, the woman turned and hurried away across the square. Kara smiled to herself as she pushed the flower into the brim of her sunhat and caught up with the others.

They sat in the shade outside a kafenion at the bottom of the square and Leo ordered four beers. The waiter reminded Kara of Jake Andrews, and for a moment she wondered what he was doing right then – if he was hauling in nets, or unloading a catch at Hayborough harbour, or if he was back home already in Elmwick, gazing out to sea with those deep eyes of his that were heavy with the weight of loss.

Marion seemed subdued, hungover, hiding behind huge sunglasses and a wide-brimmed hat. Philipe and Leo were talking about an artist they both knew, wondering idly if he still lived in the next village, if they should drive over and see him.

Kara drank her beer quickly and stood up.

'I'm going to buy some postcards and stamps,' she said.

'I'll come with you,' said Marion.

'No need – I'd like a little time on my own. I'll see you all back here in half an hour.'

She walked across to the cigarette kiosk and picked out a handful of cards: sunsets over the bay, Greek cats sitting in taverna doorways, stretched out on whitewashed walls.

She wandered through the alleyways for a while and sat down in the shade beneath a large olive tree. She wrote her cards to Mam and Louise first, full of breezy lies and rows of exclamation marks. And then the difficult card to Marty. She told him that the other students were a joy to work with, that the island was beautiful, that her painting was going well. That she missed him.

She didn't mention Leo.

Kara slipped the cards into her bag, still thinking about Marty – or more precisely, feeling guilty that she hadn't thought of Marty at all until she'd bought the postcards. She looked down at the signet ring on her right hand, glinting in the sun. Then she reminded herself that he tried to trick her, to get her pregnant, to tie her to him, and she pressed her hand against her still-flat stomach as if she'd be able to tell by touch whether she was pregnant or not. She knew she would have to do a test as soon as she got home, but for now she would do her best to forget about it.

She took out one of the spare cards and printed Marty's address on it. Then before she could change her mind, she quickly scrawled a message.

'All going well here. I've been thinking about us a lot since I left, and I've decided it's better to end things now. I know it won't work out – we're just too different. I hope you can forgive me.'

She knew it was trite, clichéd, that he didn't deserve it, yet nevertheless she put it in the postbox at the end of the street before she walked back down to the square.

EIGHT

Marion and Philipe were still in bed at ten o'clock the next morning, and Kara and Leo went down to the bay on their own. He showed her where to find the best shells, just around the next headland, and found a family of tortoises at the foot of the hillside. He held one of the babies aloft, tiny and beautifully marked, its stubby legs clawing the air.

It was the first time they'd been alone together since they arrived. After Marion's revelation the first evening, Kara had expected Leo to take her to one side, apologise for lying to her. But he'd said nothing.

He put the tortoise gently back into the scrub and opened his arms wide, gesturing around the bay.

'Welcome to Lyros! Did you know that the island is named after a goddess? Lyros asked her father if she could be turned into a dove for a single day so she could see how beautiful the island looked from above. But when she swooped back down she was killed by a stray arrow, fired by her own father as he hunted in the woods. They say the water is saltier here than anywhere else in the islands, because the sea filled up with his tears.

'What about your name, Kara? Where does it come from? It sounds like the name of a mythical goddess.'

'My father chose it. I'm named after two things – the Kara Sea in the Siberian Arctic, and Sakara, the guardian sprite from the *Stories of the Northernmost Sea*. She lived at the other side of the sea, "where the cold fish shiver", watching over shipwrecked sailors to make sure they had a safe passage to heaven, carrying them into the clouds in fishing nets spun from her flaming red hair.'

'And where are your wings?' he asked, laughing.

'I had wings once,' she said. 'My da made them from the feathers we collected on our walks on the cliff tops. He joined the quills with thin wire and then fastened the layers together with more wire and slender lathes of wood. He attached blue ribbons to them that tied over my shoulders and around my waist. I wore an old white dress of my gran's that reached the floor, with a tiara from my princess outfit.'

'I think you're still a very beautiful sprite, Sakara.'

Kara felt foolish all of a sudden, sure she'd said too much, that he would find her childish.

She pointed to the tiny island out in the bay and asked him if he'd ever been across to it.

'No, but we'll go there this afternoon.'

Leo hired a small motorboat from Katerina's brother and took her across to the island. When she jumped aboard, he held out his hand to steady her, and she thought of Da's rough hand in hers as she scrambled onto the Canny Lass in the shallows. She only went out in the coble with him occasionally, as Mam disapproved. Canny Lass was old and patched up and, to her mother's mind, unsafe. She had been Da's grandfather's boat, and had languished on land for a dozen years or more before he'd inherited her. He always promised Evie he'd stay in sight of the shore when Kara was with him. She loved curling up on the old Persian rug in the tiny makeshift cabin, with a flask of coffee and one of Da's doorstop corned beef and chutney sandwiches. She liked to watch the shore from the sea, to see their tiny cottage in the distance, the smoke rising from the boathouse chimney, the seagulls swooping and circling, their calls like crying cats as they followed the boats in the hope of stealing fish. Yet she knew Da preferred to be further out at sea on the trawler he skippered, the Mary Belle, out so far that there was nothing but sea in every direction. He told her how beautiful it was at night when the sparks of the town disappeared into the blackness, and the sea and the sky became one. It was only after dark when you understood your smallness, your insignificance in the galaxy.

And though the blue Ionian was unlike the bleak North Sea, the boat still took her back to her childhood. Kara's seaside had become amusement arcades, dodgems, waltzers, hanging out at the Quay Bar and Charelli's, ordering milky coffees and ice cream sundaes, choosing the coolest songs on the jukebox to impress teenage boys. She had cast aside the rock pools filled with intricately patterned starfish, which Da told her had been plucked from the night sky to light mermaids' houses, and sea anemones which he claimed were flowers from their gardens. Kara had collected them in her bucket along with winkles and seaweed, and after Da admired them she returned them carefully to the pools, holding the starfish gently between her fingers, their tentacles waving gracefully until they were back beneath the water, scrambling for the safety of the weed and the shade of the rocks. She loved the deep blood red of the delicate anemones, couldn't resist touching them gently to feel the pull of their tentacles. She filled her empty bucket time and time again with shells and pebbles, carried them back to the boathouse and lined them up on the bleached wood of the window ledges. Da had a big book called *Treasures of the Seashore*, and she would make tiny labels showing the names of her shells: cockles, mussels, moon snails, limpets, whelks, clams. Sometimes she'd find lumps of sea coal, as light as balsa wood, occasionally split down the centre to reveal their shiny black hearts.

When they reached the island, Kara watched Leo paint and sketch, capturing everything she didn't have the skill to portray herself. Leo painted the sea, fish, insects and birds, the shapes, the curves, the light and shadow, the perpetual movement. He carved driftwood into fish, tied them together with frayed lengths of rope he'd reclaimed from the water. He painted with bold, wide strokes in the colours of the olive groves, sliced and dappled with green shadow, bright with clean white sunlight. At home, colours were more muted, more gently shaded. Greece was cobalt blue, brilliant white, turquoise, cerise. Shadows were dark, light was bright. There was no grey. Leo looked at Kara and painted her too, tried to find the essence of her. He took his colours from the sea, the sky and the olive groves: she was yellow and blue, then green and grey, yet painting her seemed to frustrate him, as though there was something beneath that he couldn't capture, couldn't quite reach.

She told him she wanted to be a poet and a painter, and he laughed.

'Which, Kara, the artist or the writer?'

'I want to be both. Why should I have to choose?'

'You don't. You can be everything. You can fly like a bird and swim like a fish.'

He packed away his paints and sketchbooks, took her hand as they waded out to the boat. Yet on the way back she could only think about how she might be pregnant. Then all her choices would be taken away from her.

That evening they went out on their own to a nightclub in the town. The dance floor was outside beneath a trellis of vines, lit only with fairy lights. Leo held her so close she hardly dared to breathe. Under the dark sky, his was the only face she could see. He pressed his cheek to hers, and she saw the curve of his neck, the way his hair flicked over the white collar of his shirt, the tan of his skin. She had never danced like this before. Back home they went to the rock nightclub in Hayborough, where she danced in a group with Louise and the other girls.

The DJ in the Greek nightclub played the songs her mother liked, the songs she always sang along to on the radio. Kara had always thought them soppy and sentimental, but now they took on new meanings. The last record of the evening was Nilsson's 'Without You'. She remembered Mam buying it the year after Da's accident, playing it over and over again when Kara was in bed. Yet Kara knew it would mean something different to her now, that she'd find her mother's copy and play it in her bedroom when she returned home.

Leo told her she was beautiful and she believed him. They sat together in the corner of the club; she could feel each of his fingers entwined with hers. Her senses were heightened, every touch was a flash of static, a rush of heat, the sensation of something molten at her core.

She was sure he would ask her to his room that night, yet when they arrived back Philipe was still sitting on the terrace with a bottle of Metaxa, slightly drunk, demanding male company. He was adamant that Leo joined him, and Kara fell asleep to the sound of their voices echoing around the villa in the pine-scented air.

NINE

The following afternoon, Leo borrowed Philipe's car and they drove to a tiny cove at the other side of the island. Kara admired the polished wood worry beads that hung from the rearview mirror, and he lifted them down and closed her hand around them.

'Always remember today, Kara.'

They stopped at the top of steep cypress-clad cliffs, narrow steps leading down to the clear water. Around the promontory the cliffs were rockier, birds nested on the precarious ledges, their cries snatched away by the breeze. Kara recalled carrying her grandfather's old binoculars around her neck, climbing up the paths from Elmwick Bay to watch the terns and gulls. Da once found an unbroken pale blue egg, abandoned and half-hidden in bracken. Kara carried it home wrapped in a handkerchief, held it up against the light of her bedside lamp, trying to make out the half-formed bird; a bird that would never hear the wind or see the endless sky, would never swoop and dive, or soar on the currents, or take in the glitter of the sea and the roll of a hill in a single moment. Yet there was nothing inside except albumen and yolk, and she was secretly relieved.

Leo took Kara's hand and steadied her as they scrambled down the rocky steps to the soft sand. She gasped at the curve of gold, the light dancing on the water.

'It's perfect isn't it? The only sandy beach on the

island.'

He took off his T-shirt and shorts, ran straight down to the sea, splashing through the shallows, swimming out a short way before turning and waving.

'Come into the water, sea sprite!'

Kara turned and scanned the cliff tops, but there was no one around. They were totally alone. She stepped out of her sundress and ran into the sea after him, plunging beneath the water as soon as she could. She was suddenly shy. He swam back towards her, and they stood facing each other, his arm around her waist.

He kissed her forehead, then ducked under the water and grabbed her leg. She shrieked with laughter as she tumbled over, and when he resurfaced, a thousand droplets of bright water arced through the air, a rainbow of diamonds over her head. In that moment of pure joy she knew she'd been wrong to have any doubts about him. Leo had brought her here to this place, had shown her that everything could be beautiful again. Perhaps he could save her.

They swam across the bay, then lay together on the sand, their wet skin glistening, their eyes closed, until the sun dipped low.

'Come on,' Leo said at last. 'We'd better get back before dinner or they'll be sending out a search party.'

They drove back in silence. When their arms accidentally touched, skin on skin, Kara flinched away from the heat as though she feared it would burn her. By the time they arrived at the villa the sky was dark, the lamps already switched on above the terrace. Leo pressed his finger to Kara's lips, led her round to the side entrance. They slipped into his room together and he threw open the windows onto their private garden.

'No one will look for us here,' he whispered.

They took cushions out onto the veranda, Leo made love to her in the lemon-scented garden, illuminated by fireflies, and when it was over he ran his hands over every inch of her skin and kissed each of her fingers in turn. In the dark their tangled limbs blended into one; a single shade of pale. She held her arm against his to show him.

'In the dark all cats are grey,' he said. 'Yet in the light of the morning you will turn back into a tortoiseshell kitten and I'll be revealed as a grumpy old tuxedo tomcat.'

Kara shook her head and laughed. 'No, we're destined to mate forever, we will be faithful creatures like snow cranes or wolves.'

He said nothing in reply, but stood up to fetch his cigarettes, and when he returned he walked over to the veranda railing and gazed out across the garden. As he stood there he was almost a stranger to her, yet in such a short time she'd allowed him to become everything that mattered.

They stayed outside until the stars were high above them, drinking a bottle of rough, chilled retsina that Leo had taken from Katerina's fridge.

'There's something about retsina that I love,' he said. 'It tastes exactly like the scent of the evening air.'

The fireflies had dimmed, but other night creatures flew around them in the darkness: moths fluttering against the lit windows, tiny bats criss-crossing the garden.

'For the last three evenings I've waited up for you,' Kara said, 'hoping you'd come to my room.'

He smiled.

'And every evening I've waited for you too, left the windows open, listened out for the air rushing through your wings. But anticipation always makes the first kiss sweeter. Perhaps it's better that we spent some time together first, got to know each other a little?'

He lit two cigarettes and handed one to her, stretched out on the cushions, looking up at the stars. He talked about art, poetry, quoted Louis MacNeice, told her the tragic story of a famous artist's muse. Yet although this was everything she'd imagined, Kara felt suddenly out of her depth. It was like a vivid dream where everything was heightened, sharply in focus, yet just out of reach. She heard herself agreeing with his views, trying to sound more sophisticated and knowledgeable than she felt. She was conscious of acting a part, of trying to be whoever Leo wanted her to be. When they made love she'd felt confident, certain of everything, yet when he talked to her like this she didn't know who he was or who she was trying to be. And in every conversation, Leo made it appear he was revealing more than he was, so it was only later when Kara realised how little he'd said about himself. He asked her so many questions that she scarcely noticed she'd learned nothing about him in return.

The following afternoon Marion and Philipe insisted that Leo and Kara went into the town with them. They wandered around the alleyways, browsed in the shops, swifts darting low over their heads, back and forth beneath the eaves where they were nesting. Marion picked up olive-wood spoons, embroidered shawls, silver bangles, and afterwards they found a quayside cafe, ordered coffees, and pastries drenched in honey.

A dirty white cat, slender as a lathe, sprawled beneath the shade of an olive tree eating a dusty fish. Time seemed to stand still as they watched it tear the fish apart with its tiny white teeth, and no one spoke. Marion appeared to be nursing another hangover, snapping at Philipe for no reason, yet he shrugged it off good-naturedly.

'Marion, I've given you everything I have. I've shown you loyalty, I've never messed around with other women – yet still you give me grief!'

'Maybe that's your problem, Philipe,' said Leo, laughing. 'I have no admiration for fidelity and commitment – they quickly make a love affair stale and sterile. I can love with more tenderness, more passion, if I know the relationship will only be fleeting. In fact I don't like the word "relationship", I prefer the word "affair", because it sounds so much more fun. Love should be rapid, intense, a transient thing.'

Kara laughed along with Philipe and Marion, pretending to agree, yet something inside her turned cold. Despite feeling out of her depth, she'd been confident of Leo's love, sure that he wanted her, and her alone. He'd never once mentioned his estranged wife, and Kara found it easy to pretend she didn't exist, had been untroubled by the thought of her until now. Yet she wasn't sure about anything. It felt like a game, a game in which she didn't understand how to make her next move, hadn't grasped exactly how it worked, hadn't learned the rules.

She fingered the worry beads tied around her wrist and suddenly noticed her right hand was bare. Marty's signet ring was no longer on her middle finger. She examined her hand, as though she expected it to reappear at any moment. She couldn't remember when she'd last seen it. It must have slipped off her finger in the sea the previous afternoon. Kara started to scrabble in her handbag, just in case it had fallen in there, yet she knew it was unlikely. She'd wanted to give it back to Marty when she got home, and it would sound like a lie if she had to tell him she'd lost it.

Marion noticed her panic.

'What's the matter, Kara? Have you lost something?'

'My signet ring – I can't even think when I last saw it.'

'Was it valuable?'

'No, not really. It was gold, but nothing too expensive.'

'But a gift I expect, and of sentimental value if I know you young girls? Don't worry, Leo will buy you something much better to replace it – won't you, darling?'

'Oh no, no, he doesn't need to do that,' Kara stuttered. 'It wasn't important at all.'

'Nonsense! Leo, take her over to that lovely little jeweller's on the corner – tell Spiros I sent you. We'll meet you at Fokos's afterwards for cocktails? Let's stay out, make a night of it? What do you say?'

By ten o'clock everyone was drunk on a mixture of cocktails, wine and Metaxa. They had ordered a meze of olives, dips and bread, yet only Kara had touched it, and the alcohol had gone straight to their heads.

She kept looking down at the silver ring on her left hand, a dolphin wrapped around her finger, its head and tail overlapping. Leo had chosen it, yet he'd been pushed into buying it, and he made it clear it had no significance.

'It's just a simple token to remind you of your trip, Kara.'

She'd nodded and smiled, holding out her left hand, wondering if he'd understood the significance of placing it on her ring finger.

'Of course – thank you. It's beautiful and I'll treasure it.'

A man at the next table began to sing, something mournful, soulful, a song that everyone in the taverna appeared to know. He stood up when they clapped and launched straight into another song, sadder than the first.

'*Nissiotika*,' Philipe whispered in her ear. 'Traditional island songs.'

Kara loved the raw emotion, the passion, the way the Greek words told her whatever story she wanted to hear.

When she got up, her head swam. She wove her way through the tables, holding on to chair backs, staggering against the wall. As she went through the main door into the ladies' she noticed a tall blonde woman going into one of the cubicles in front of her. The woman half-turned as she heard the door opening behind her. Kara gasped. This time she was sure: it was Lola.

She stayed by the basins and waited for her, hoping that no one else would come in. When the cubicle door opened she was ready to speak, had planned what to say, but the words came out slurred. The woman glanced at Kara with disgust, pushed past her to wash her hands.

After she'd left, Kara leant her forehead against the cool marble tiles and cried. The woman had hardly resembled Lola Armitage at all, yet she'd been so sure. The past refused to leave her alone, would never stop tricking her. Sometimes it called so loudly Kara could hear nothing else. Yet Da and Lola were both gone for good, and she knew she had to find a way to accept things as they were.

She splashed cold water on her face and went back out into the bar, and when they returned to the villa she followed Leo into his room and stayed there until Katerina knocked on the door to ask if they wanted any lunch.

TEN

The rest of their time in Greece passed the same way.

Leo and Kara painted and sketched in the mornings, made love in the afternoons, the room shuttered against the heat, an ancient fan whirring loudly in the corner. In the evenings they drank wine and made small talk with Philipe and Marion.

Yet in their last few days together, Leo became more distant. It was as though the closer they became physically, the further he retreated emotionally. He avoided being alone with her outside the bedroom, always leaping straight out of bed after they'd made love, rushing to shower and change, to find Philipe and talk about his recent trip to Monaco, about old friends, about art and politics. And in the mornings, Leo stopped going down to the cove to paint. He suddenly found errands to run, or went out early with Philipe in the car, driving into the hills in search of the artist they'd talked about. They would bring back small gifts for Kara and Marion: rose honey bought at the roadside, paper twists of almonds, fresh figs, silver earrings in the shape of fish. Yet it was clear to Kara that these were gifts from Philipe rather than Leo.

Kara still told herself that everything was fine, and when Leo wasn't there she swam up and down the pool, or went down to the bay to sketch on her own – anything to avoid idle chatter with Marion. She didn't want to hear the things she knew Marion would say, didn't want her advice about how unwise it was to fall for Leo, how she must forget him when they went home, how she must treat it as nothing more than a holiday romance.

But when they were together in Leo's room, Kara forgot about Marion and Philipe, about her doubts, about how little time they had left on Lyros. When they made love, Leo was as attentive as ever, and on the afternoon of their last day she told him she loved him.

The words were barely audible, whispered so softly she might never have said them, but she knew he'd heard them, felt the perceptible pause in his rhythm. He didn't reply, didn't acknowledge she'd spoken, and in the heavy heat of the afternoon her love hung in the air for only a moment before being swallowed by the whir of the fan.

Kara knew those three words hadn't been a declaration of her own feelings so much as a plea for confirmation. They were closer to a question, words borne of a desperate need to be cherished. She wasn't making a statement; she was asking Leo if he loved her.

And though she tried to hold on to those last hours in Lyros, they slipped away from her like the receding tide. She wasn't sure what would happen after they arrived back in Hayborough, and when she thought about doing a pregnancy test it weighed heavy in the pit of her stomach.

When they left, Philipe and Marion drove them to the ferry at first light, Marion kissing and hugging Kara through the car window as Leo took their cases from the boot.

'Come back next summer, Kara!' she called, as they drove away.

'I will!' she shouted, and she stood by her case and waved until they were out of sight.

When she turned round Leo had already disappeared into the waiting room.

The Friday they flew home was the night of Louise and Paul's engagement party at the village hall in Elmwick. All their college tutors had been invited, including Leo.

When the taxi dropped Kara off at home it was already nearly seven, and she rushed upstairs to get ready to go out. She was relieved she had no time to talk to Mam right then. She didn't want to be quizzed about her trip, or about her postcard to Marty. She knew her mother would be annoyed with her for ending it with him, and it was something she couldn't face right then. She tried to call Louise to find out how Marty had taken it, but her mother said she'd already gone down to the village hall.

It was a beautiful evening. The dipping sun cast long shadows across the fields, deepening the warm gold of the drystone walls, and Kara could smell the sweet musk of the heather. She walked to the end of the lane to catch the bus, watching the swallows as they circled the pond in Tom Reid's field, reminding her of the pair of swifts that swooped over the swimming pool at the villa in Lyros.

She wore red velvet flares and a top made from diaphanous cotton, dip-dyed in a rainbow of pastel shades. She left her hair loose. It was so long now she could almost sit on it, and in the evening sunlight it shone as glossy as a newly split conker.

There was already quite a crowd in the village hall, yet there was no one Kara knew well. Paul was talking to some of the Whitby bikers, Louise was nowhere to be seen. The music was loud, and three girls were dancing to Blondie. Kara took two glasses of champagne from a table by the door and drank them one after the other, then bought a bottle of beer and sat down in a corner so she could watch everyone arriving.

Leo walked in ten minutes later and sat down near the makeshift bar with one of the other tutors. Kara assumed he hadn't seen her, so she went over with the excuse of asking him to dance. She grabbed his hand and pulled him up, ignoring his apologetic shrug to the other tutor, his reluctance as he followed her to the middle of the room. When the DJ noticed his first couple of the evening he quickly faded out Blue Oyster Cult and dropped 'Your Song' by Elton John onto the turntable. The girls groaned and walked off, leaving Leo and Kara in the centre of the village hall on their own. Kara reached for Leo's hand and he put his other arm around her waist, yet she could hardly hear the music, knowing everyone in the room was watching, that Leo would be annoyed. She lowered her eyes and concentrated on not standing on his toes. She felt dizzy with their secret, her heart lurching every time the door opened in case Marty walked in. Now she was back home she felt bad about what she'd done to him, yet she knew if she hadn't ended it she would have felt even worse.

When she'd arrived at the party she'd been impatient for the evening to start, wanting it to be over quickly so she could be alone with Leo, imagining them making love in the dunes under the northern stars. Yet something in his face that evening made her doubt everything, and now she wanted the dance to last forever, to hold him like this, suspended in time. That way she wouldn't have to move forward, wouldn't have to see Marty, do a pregnancy test, hear Leo say that it was never going to work out between them.

But it seemed like only moments before the song came to an end. Leo led her off the dance floor, pointed to a spare table and asked if she wanted another drink. She said yes, and while he was at the bar she went out to the toilets so she could check if there was anyone she knew at the picnic tables. When she came out of the cubicle one of the upper sixth girls caught her eye in the mirror.

'You looked pretty close there, you and Leo Chapman? Be careful, Kara, he's not what he seems. Keep it to yourself, but my mother knows one of the teachers at his school in Oxford, and he told her Leo had to leave his job because of the rumour of a relationship with one of his students last summer. Nothing was ever proven, which is why he's still teaching – the girl herself denied it.'

Kara shrugged. 'No need to worry, there's nothing going on,' she said.

'Well I hope for your sake that's true.'

The girl dried her hands and turned to leave, then stopped as she reached the door.

'And I hope you know his wife is pregnant?'

As she walked away, Kara's head swam. Every step she took along the corridor was an effort, her feet as heavy as bricks – in those few words everything had spun out of orbit.

When she walked back into the hall, Leo was nowhere to be seen. She pushed her way through the crowd and out of the back door into the car park. He was sitting in his car, the window wound down. She could see the glow of his cigarette, his arm resting on the sill.

'Leo?'

He said nothing for a few moments, stared straight ahead towards the sea, but when he turned to look at her his eyes confirmed everything she'd feared.

He started to repeat the same things in a low, urgent voice. He would say goodbye now, not drag it out. She must go to university and forget about him.

'We had fun didn't we? I don't want to hurt you, Kara, but what did you expect would happen when we came back? Surely you can see that I could never be with you? I'm thirty-two and you're only just seventeen. And I have a wife, you always knew that.'

As he talked, his eyes glittered like glass. He was already disengaging from her, his expression an embarrassed smirk she hadn't seen before: guilty, yet not sorry. When he finished speaking she stayed silent for a moment, then leaned forward into the car. In Greece, Kara had felt powerless, had been consumed by something she'd called love; and that love had felt real and true in the heady, perfumed air. Yet here, in her home village, the truth had been laid bare, and she wasn't going to let him drive away without letting him know she understood that truth.

'Yes, I knew you had a wife, but I thought you were separated, that it was all over between you. And what about Greece? Does your wife believe in the Philipe

80

Patou Art Foundation too?'

'Of course she does – how else do you think I can get away like that?'

'So you've done this before?'

'Kara, can't you see it's complicated?'

'Yeah, I'm sure it's complicated. I suppose the fact that your wife is pregnant is what makes it *really* complicated?'

She turned on her heel and started walking slowly back towards the hall.

Then she remembered the dolphin ring. She pulled it off her finger and threw it at his car, heard the satisfying 'ding' as it glanced off the bonnet.

Leo called after her, but it was half-hearted, and when she didn't answer he switched on the engine and reversed out of the car park. She watched him drive away, and it was only as his car turned the corner out of sight that she could see everything clearly for the first time.

She'd been nothing more than a small fish for him to toy with – so easily caught. He'd lured her with his fancy bait, reeled her in, slowly slowly, softly softly, and now he'd thrown her back. Everything about their relationship had been shallow artifice. The romantic Greek villa, the clever talk, the false friends. A fake world.

As she stood at the door she could hear the music and laughter inside, the sea whispering to her below. The last of the light was still holding out in the mid-summer sky, yet Kara saw a bruised and bloodshot sundown; the colours she would have once thought glorious now reminded her of wounds. Then she remembered the night she'd sat in the playground with Louise. Everything had come sharply into focus in that one moment of clarity. It arrived from nowhere on a warm breeze, and they'd glimpsed a future where everything was guaranteed to be good.

She knew she couldn't let this ending define her: it must somehow be turned into a beginning.

But she wouldn't think about that now.

Kara drank two more of the free glasses of champagne as she waited for the barman to bring her a double vodka and tonic. She pressed the cold glass against her forehead and stood just inside the door, watching all the Hayborough sixth-form girls. They were drunk, laughing, shouting to each other above the noise of the music, exotic creatures in their Indian tops scattered with mirrors that caught the light. Most of the girls from her school had the veneer of middle-class money, of single-sex education. They had a sense of entitlement, so sure that life would take them elsewhere, somewhere better than this one-trick town. They flirted with the trawler lads and the bikers, flattered them with their attention – amusing themselves with their 'bit of rough' before they left for city universities. Kara was suddenly angry with them for making everything a game.

She could see the stark contrast between these girls and the Hayborough biker crowd in their leathers and spike-heeled boots. They were down-to-earth, had a confidence rooted in hard knocks and real-life experience, were well used to jockeying for position with the boys. They were girls who didn't suffer fools, who would never have been tricked by Leo Chapman any more than they would try to trick anyone themselves.

Then Kara watched Louise dancing with Paul, leaning in, reaching up on tiptoe to whisper in his ear. Paul caught her eye and frowned briefly before turning his attention back to Louise again. She was suddenly jealous of what they had, couldn't bear to see them so secure in the knowledge of their future together. And although it wasn't a future she wanted for herself, at that moment she would have given anything to be Lou, to have the love of someone like Paul: the boy next door. Louise and Paul were the realest thing in the room, there was no artifice.

She laughed to herself, a hollow laugh, when she realised she'd had exactly that herself. She'd had Marty, who would have done anything for her, who'd always been patient even when he didn't understand her sadness or anger, her sudden irrational fears. Even though she knew in her heart they would never have made it, she'd thrown him away as if he were nothing. Ended their relationship with a postcard.

Something within her broke. She squeezed her way between the dancers and tapped Louise on the shoulder, wanting to take her away from Paul, wanting to tell her about Leo, to explain about Marty, to cry on her shoulder like the old days. Louise followed her off the dance floor.

'Kara, how was your trip? You're so tanned! Sorry I haven't spoken to you yet, I've been monopolised by . . .' She paused when she saw Kara's face. 'What's the matter? Are you okay? You look as pale as a ghost.'

'Leo's dumped me. His wife's pregnant. Did you know?'

'Of course I knew, I thought you did too. This isn't news you're telling me. That's why I couldn't understand what you were doing going to Greece with him. I hoped you had more sense than to take it that far, but when Marty got your card I realised you were dafter than I thought. And what about Marty, Kara? I'm sure you didn't mean to hurt him so badly, yet you led him on, you weren't fair to him, and now he's heartbroken. How could you just end it like that, with a postcard for God's sake – didn't he at least deserve a conversation? It's Paul who's having to pick up the pieces, make him realise it isn't his fault. Where do you think he is tonight? He should be here with us, celebrating our engagement, but he's at home on his own. You hadn't even thought about that had you, hadn't even wondered where he was? Leo, Leo, Leo – that's all that seems to matter.'

'Marty hasn't guessed about Leo has he? No one must ever know.'

'You see, even now that's all you're thinking about. And what about Leo's wife, Kara, what about her? It will be better for everyone when you leave and go to university.'

'Well don't worry, Lou, it's all over with Leo. And you won't have that long to wait until I've gone for good!'

She turned away, but Louise grabbed her arm.

'I've never said anything to you about it before, Kara, but I know the rumour about your Da – and about that girl. And I know what you did, how you almost lost your life. My mother heard it all from somewhere a long time ago, but she only told me last year. I wanted to tell you I knew, yet it just seemed too hard. I've never said a word to anyone, I've never gossiped. I love you,

Kara, and I'm so sorry you still don't know the truth about your da. Maybe you'll find what you really want when you leave here. Yet somehow I doubt it, because I think you're trying to replace someone irreplaceable, and nobody else will ever love you enough.'

Kara pulled away from her.

'You don't know anything about it.'

She started to cross the room, stumbling between the dancers until she found herself standing below the whirling glitter ball. She stopped, eyes blurry with tears as everyone stepped around her, then a hand reached for hers and pulled her off the dance floor to the back of the hall.

It was Jake Andrews. She looked in the mirror on the far wall, saw herself as he would see her, face as pale as Ophelia in the weeds, dark eyes glittering with something desperate.

'Are you okay?'

She nodded and went over to the bar, switching on a smile. Jake followed her and squeezed between the crowd to stand at the table at her side.

'I'll get that,' he said as she picked up a bottle of Newcastle Brown.

She looked him up and down.

'So, Jake,' she said, 'it seems as though you're here to save me again!'

She laughed a little too loudly, tripping over a chair leg as they walked away from the bar.

'Come outside, Kara – you need some fresh air.'

She laughed again and took a swig of her beer.

'Tell me, Jake, what do you do with yourself when you're not waiting to rescue fallen angels? Do you sit in your cottage watching the sea from your bedroom window?'

'I'm a trawler skipper,' he said. 'So I guess I'm always watching the sea.'

'My da was a trawler skipper too. He drowned seven years ago. And I still miss him.'

She took his hand and led him outside to sit on the harbour wall. They sat in silence, side by side, looking up at the wheeling stars, until eventually he spoke.

'When my brother died they offered me his job in the steelworks. But I didn't want to be Billy's shadow, everyone comparing us, perhaps wishing he was still there and I wasn't. And my da, waiting for me to come home from my shift, sometimes wishing it was Billy coming back instead. I didn't want to hang my star on my brother's peg. So I took a job on the trawlers, and now I'm a skipper. One day you'll have to let go of the past, Kara. You need to give yourself permission to grab your own star and make it shine for you.'

ELEVEN

When Kara woke up she was in Jake's bed. He opened his eyes as though he'd sensed her watching him, and when she started to speak he pressed his finger to her lips. They lay together in silence and watched each other appear, inch by inch, out of the grey dawn. In the half-light, the edgeland between night and day, Jake's skin was ghostly, as if he were underwater. He smiled, reached for her hand beneath the covers, and Kara stared at him as though seeing him for the first time. She'd always been aware of some kind of understanding between them – known they were kindred spirits, troubled soulmates, sensed something of their shared vulnerability. Yet until that morning she'd never really looked at him properly in a physical sense, and she could see that the picture she'd carried of him in her head had never been in focus. All she knew was that when she was with Jake she was safe. No, it was more than that: she was home. Jake was her harbour.

After the dance, Kara had wanted to give herself up to him as though nothing else mattered, had wanted to make him love her in the only way she knew how. Everything she cared about had been taken from her, and she needed something, someone – anything – to fill the void, to drown out the noise of the loneliness. Yet Jake wouldn't let her, he held her at arm's length, stopped her from cheapening the bright, pure thing that connected them. She could see in his eyes that he wasn't fooled by her, that he understood the emptiness inside her, that he knew she was broken, grief and love pouring slowly out of her.

When they arrived at the cottage she stayed silent, tried not to show her surprise at where he lived. She had never been back inside this house since her and Mam moved out to High Rigg. She held back for a moment before she went through the door, but Jake didn't appear to notice. Once they were inside she wanted to examine everything. She walked around the room, running her fingers along window ledges and walls as though mapping out the space, storing it in her head for future recall.

Jake watched her the following morning as she gazed out of the kitchen window at the dark sea, the horizon marked by fishing boats far out from the shore.

'It's wonderful to be so close to the sea,' she said. 'To watch the light alter throughout the day, to see the water change from grey to ink and the sky deepen to fire. I've lived close to the sea all my life and I could never leave. Oh listen to me now – the sea, the sea, the sky, the sky,' she said softly. 'I sound like my da.'

She looked sad for a moment, then her face cleared.

Jake saw her expression change, took her hand and held it in both of his, as if wanting to hold onto her before she could be reclaimed by the other world in her head.

'It's a beautiful morning, Kara, a great day for a spin out on the bike?'

She shook her head. 'I need to go home today, I want to see Louise, to sort some things out. But I'll call you. I will.'

'If you need a place to stay, some time on your own, then you can come over here whenever you like. It's quiet, you could read and swim every day, and I'd be at work most of the time, out of your way.'

Kara smiled. 'I might just take you up on that.'

'Great – just turn up, whenever. There's always a key under the mat at the back.'

He kissed the top of her head and hugged her tightly. It was as though he already understood what she needed, knew that if she came back it would be for herself rather than for him, yet he accepted that.

Kara raced to the bus stop, the mirrors on her handbag catching the sun. She had borrowed Jake's toothbrush, run a comb through her hair, wiped the stray flecks of mascara from under her eyes.

When she got home her mam seemed distracted. Kara had been worried that she would question her about the party, about staying out all night, would somehow have found out about Leo or her fight with Louise. Yet when Kara sat down at the kitchen table, her mother just nodded and smiled as her daughter talked, barely glancing across as she busied herself making toast.

She hardly looked her in the eye, and when Kara went upstairs to collect the laundry she noticed the photo of Da was no longer by her mother's bedside. She opened the cabinet drawer and found it there, facedown. She lifted it out. Underneath, there was a box of condoms, open and half-empty. She dropped the photo onto the glass top with a clatter as Mam came into the room.

She blushed, taking in the scene in a single glance.

'Kara . . . I was going to tell you. It's Tom. Tom Reid. He came over to discuss the wall repairs while you were away in London that time and we got talking. He's been lonely too since his wife passed away. It seems we have a lot in common. You'll like him, I know you will, I want you to get on . . . I like him a lot.'

'How long have you been seeing him?'

'Just a few weeks. I didn't want to tell you until I was sure it was serious.'

'Serious?'

'Kara, it's seven years since Da died. Seven years. And for that seven years I've been totally alone. I've had no one. I'll never forget him, and no one can truly replace him, but I'm only thirty-nine years old. I didn't put the photo away because I don't love your da any more, I put it away out of respect. For both Tom and Da. It seemed wrong to have him watching us.'

'You didn't have "no one", you had me.'

'I didn't though, did I? You were your father's child from the day you were born. I hardly got a look in. Your da loved you so much – unconditionally and without limit. And so do I . . . '

Kara couldn't bear to see the sadness in Mam's eyes, couldn't face the possibility that she was the cause of it.

'I'm sorry,' she whispered. She picked up the photo and ran out of the room with it. As she reached the foot of the stairs her mother shouted after her.

'Tom's coming to dinner tonight – he's looking forward to getting to know you.'

TWELVE

Kara decided not to like Tom Reid. She knew it was petty and childish, yet she couldn't help herself. She ate her meal in silence, watched the movements of his strong weathered hands as he cut his steak and drank his red wine.

'So, Kara, your mother tells me you're off to the bright lights to study English next year?'

She nodded. 'If by "the bright lights" you mean London, then yes, I guess so,' she said.

Mam glared at her and Tom patted her hand.

'She's alright, aren't you love? You probably just want to get off and meet up with your friends instead of being stuck here with us adults.'

'I am an adult,' hissed Kara, 'and I won't be going out to see my friends just so you can get some time alone with my mother.'

She pushed her chair back and clattered up to her room, ignoring Mam's shouts from the bottom of the stairs. She grabbed her coat and bag and turned to leave again, but when she opened the door Tom was waiting for her, blocking the narrow stairwell, arms stretched out, hands firmly planted at either side.

'You should apologise to your mother, Kara. I know it's difficult for you, that you've found it hard, but it's all a long time ago now and Evie has her life to lead. She deserves to be happy.'

'You know nothing about me. Please, just leave me

alone and get out of my way.'

'Not so hasty, young lass. I know all about you. Rumours travel fast in Hayborough. I know how friendly you are with that art teacher, when he's married an' all, and her expecting. Do you think your mam would be proud of you if she knew – or your late father come to that?'

Kara stepped back into her room and slammed the door, sliding the bolt across.

'You know nothing about me! Don't ever mention my da again!'

She slumped against the wall, her heart hammering. When she heard him leave, she waited another ten minutes before tiptoeing downstairs to the parlour. She knew Tom wouldn't repeat what he'd said to her – he was still trying to impress. She made sure she could hear both their voices in the kitchen before she picked up the phone and dialled Louise's number. There was no reply.

Kara went back up to her room and lay on the bed, burying her head in Pilot's soft neck as he eyed her mournfully. She wanted to cry, but her eyes were dry and gritty and the tears refused to come. She'd managed to lose everyone she loved in the space of two weeks: Leo, Marty, Louise, and now Mam. Every one of her stories had an unhappy ending.

Louise had been the only true friend she'd ever had. After Da's accident none of her school friends had known what to say to her. They were too young to grasp the significance of her loss or understand grief. The year she started at grammar school was the same year Louise moved to the town, and she was assigned the empty desk next to Kara's. Kara knew straight away that they'd be friends. She'd always felt safe with her, it was inconceivable to think their friendship would ever end.

The first time she slept with Marty she hadn't meant for him to fall in love with her. It was just something she was trying out, part of a longing to be whole again. How could she have ever hoped to love him back when everything was still so confused, so open-ended, how could she move on without some kind of closure? Da had gone, yet there had been no body, no proper funeral, and she hadn't even been allowed to see the Canny Lass. Mam had sold the boat straight away, sent it on George's trailer to a fisherman up the coast – a stranger – without even emptying it of Da's belongings. It was as though her mother had wanted to keep hope alive by not saying a final goodbye to Da, yet Kara hadn't been given any choice.

The next morning, Kara gathered her things together quickly, stuffing clothes and make-up into her rucksack along with the framed photo of her and Da standing in front of the Canny Lass. As she left her bedroom she snatched the piece of Greek sea glass from her dressing table and pushed it into the pocket of her jeans. She wrote a note saying she was staying with a friend and left it on her bed before creeping downstairs. She didn't write down the address, didn't want Mam to know that Jake's house was their old cottage.

Most of the row of cottages had changed hands since they lived there. People had died, sold up, moved on, and she hadn't imagined for a minute that Jake would live at number seventeen. For some reason she still hadn't told him, hadn't wanted him to know. When he led her upstairs they'd carried on up to the attic, and she'd been relieved to find he didn't sleep in her parents' bedroom. Someone had installed a window in the roof and Jake's bed was directly underneath it, looking up at the stars.

Kara thought of the nights she'd sat in her bedroom window counting those same stars. She tried to map them, number them, filling endless pages of her sketchbook with intricate patterns of hundreds of tiny dots. On clear winter nights there were so many stars that they overlapped and interlaced, filled the sky with a solid expanse of milky luminance. She never became tired of gazing up at them, and sometimes she was almost stiff with cold when she heard Da climbing the stairs to check on her.

If he caught Kara at the window, Da would sit at her side counting the stars with her, teaching her the names of constellations. At weekends they would go out together after dark, wrapped in scarves and hats, climb up to the top of the cliffs and lie on their backs watching the Milky Way wheeling above them.

When she arrived at the cottage, Jake was out on his motorbike, and she found a back-door key under the mat as he'd promised. It was a dull day, too cold to go swimming, the early morning sun hidden behind sullen clouds, the sea grey and moody.

Kara considered looking round upstairs while Jake was out, but something stopped her from going into her old room when she was in the house alone. She made herself a mug of tea and stood at the kitchen window. In the distance she could make out a tractor dragging a coble up the slipway on a low trailer, and the shape of the old boathouse. It looked like someone was using it again at last. She remembered the times she'd seen Lola Armitage there after their first meeting with her on the beach. Kara would often walk on to the boathouse after school, and sometimes she'd find Lola there talking to Da, leaning against the side of the shed while he tinkered with his motorbike, or sitting on the edge of the slipway with her sketchbook and pencils, her long legs swinging, watching him mend the nets. When she saw Kara she would jump on her bicycle and ride away without saying a word.

The day before the accident had been a Thursday, and Kara was sent home from school early because the boiler had broken down. Mam was still at the library, so she went to find Da. She found him in the front shed, patching up the Canny Lass's hull. The stove was lit in the back and she took two custard creams from the tin and settled at Da's workbench with her homework. She had a new craft project to start, and she pulled out her roll of sugar paper and took the scissors from the drawer.

She jumped when the side door flew open and Lola walked in without knocking. She looked surprised to see Kara there, and at first she stood in silence, unsure what to do or say.

'Is Ged in?' she asked at last. 'What are you doing here anyway, shouldn't you be at school?'

Kara shook her head, but didn't answer. She stared at Lola, took in the dark smudges of eyeshadow, the tortoiseshell clip in her hair, the bold lipstick, the silver bangles that clattered noisily on her wrists.

Lola went back outside and round to the double doors at the front. Kara could hear their voices; the rhythm of Da's measured speech, the rise and fall of Lola's questions, the tinkle of her bangles as her voice became more strained. Then silence, and eventually Lola's footsteps as she walked back round the side, followed by the tick-click-tick of her bike wheels as she pushed it down the path onto the road.

Kara remembered that evening so well. She felt the same tug of fear as when they'd seen Lola on the beach, yet something told her to say nothing to Da, and she continued with her homework until he came through to help her.

Kara carried her mug of tea back over to the kitchen table. She noticed a calendar hanging on the same hook where Da always kept the RNLI one that he used to record his work shifts – the pre-dawn starts, the night fishing, those three-day weekends that Kara loved, especially when they fell in the summer holidays and they could go exploring the cliff paths together. When she looked closely she saw Jake had marked his shifts down too, and it sent a chill through her, the thought that Jake could be lost at sea, could be snatched away just like Da, could disappear without a trace. She remembered Da telling her that some fishermen never learn to swim, believing it's better to drown quickly.

She sat down at the table, choosing the same place to sit as when it had been their house. The kitchen wasn't much different to how it had been then. The old Aga was still there, and the wall cupboards Da had built were now painted a bright yellow.

She remembered the night of the accident, sitting at the kitchen table with her school project laid out on newspaper, waiting for Da to come home with the extra strong glue. The evening before, after Lola had gone, they had spread it all out on his workbench in the boathouse.

'Why are you making wings for a fish?' he asked her.

'It's for our "Faithful Creatures" project. I wanted to make a swan, but Jane got the swan. I got given the French angelfish. But angels have wings, so I'm making a half-fish, half-angel. Mrs Broadbent said it was okay.'

Da nodded to himself, took the squashed bouquets of feathers that Kara had collected, untied the string. There were gull feathers, grey and white with soft down at the quick, a mixed group of smaller feathers that were striped and spotted, two glossy black quills from a raven or rook. Da sorted them into sizes, then he divided each pile roughly in half. He laid them out around Kara's fish, starting with the smallest and building up to the longest, forming two wing-fins at the top and bottom. He stood back and looked at them critically, then nodded to himself and fetched a sheet of corrugated card. He traced a shape around Kara's paper fish before cutting the cardboard to the same size.

'Tomorrow, I'll buy a new tube of limpet sticky and we'll glue these two layers together.'

Kara laughed at their special name for superglue. Da looked up, smiling, and when their eyes met she felt something plummet inside her, the weight of something she didn't understand. It was almost a premonition, the knowledge that this was all fleeting – this love, this security, this happiness. She felt something cracking, some unaccountable sadness wash over her, yet Da didn't seem to notice. He ruffled her hair and kissed her forehead.

'Right, now we know we have enough feathers we can push each one inside a channel of the corrugated card to form the wing-fins. Tomorrow when I get the sticky, we'll make sure they're exactly as you want them and then we'll glue them in place. Now, pass me the feathers in order of size.'

She sat in silence, holding her breath, handing him the feathers one by one, looking up at the clock, knowing Mam would be cross if they were late for supper. Yet she wanted to stay there with Da forever, to be with him all the time, like the special stone she'd given him. Sometimes she asked him to show it to her, and the stone was always there in his pocket or his lunch bag, never leaving his side, just as he'd promised.

When all the feathers were in place, Da held up the card. Even part-finished, Kara could see her fish was going to be beautiful. Mongrel wings, grey and brown, striped, stippled, speckled. Kara thought they were the most glorious wing-fins she'd ever seen. Her angelfish would be able to soar above cliffs and dive deep into the ocean.

When Jake arrived back he found her sitting in the dark by the kitchen window, watching the sea, the shimmer of light on the water. He didn't ask any questions; he simply took her hand and led her upstairs without a word.

THIRTEEN

The next morning, Kara woke up alone. Through the skylight she watched wisps of cloud float across the rectangle of clear blue. It was going to be a better day.

She reached for the pile of books on the floor: the well-thumbed copies of sci-fi classics, a book on deep sea fishing, and a volume of poetry – *The Nightfishing* by W S Graham. She opened it and took in the beauty of the words, the descriptions of the sea, the weather, the salt dark. A fine pencil had been used to highlight some of the lines. Kara read those words over and over again, as though she would discover something more of Jake through their meaning, something of how he felt when he was out at sea beneath the stars. The words he'd chosen as special made her heart miss a beat; she felt as though she'd stumbled upon a secret, that he must never know she'd opened the book.

As she reached over the edge of the bed to put the books back in order she felt a sudden cramping in her abdomen. She rushed to the bathroom with her heart pounding. When she saw the blood in the toilet bowl she cried with relief, yet some part of her was crying for Marty too.

Downstairs, the kitchen was filled with sunlight. Jake had spread a bright checked cloth over the table and there was a mountain of thick toast piled up on a plate in the centre.

She leaned over to kiss him as she edged her way round the table to her seat.

'You're happy this morning!' he said. 'Jam or honey? Or there may be some marmalade somewhere.'

'Wow, I'm impressed! I'll have jam please.'

'Sorry there's only toast, but I thought we could go to Saltburn on the bike today. Take that ride I promised you? We can have a proper fish and chip lunch and I'll win loads of tat for you in the pier amusements.'

It was a rare and perfect summer's day. The sea was millpond calm, a deep deep blue, and as they drove along the edge of the moors she caught the coconut scent of late gorse flowers. The tarmac stretched away in front of them like a black ribbon, a shimmering heat haze floating like some Saharan mirage at the brow of every hill. Kara wrapped her arms around Jake's waist, felt the soft, warm leather of his jacket against her cheek.

Saltburn was busy with a bright throng of day-trippers, over-eager to enjoy themselves, hardly able to believe their luck with the weather. Dogs raced in and out of the sea, parents steered toddlers in sun bonnets down to the shallows. Kara and Jake walked through the arcade and along the pier. When they came back again he took her hand and led her to the tuppenny falls. He tapped the glass above a cheap gold-coloured cocktail ring that teetered atop a thick wedge of coins at the very edge, told Kara to guard it while he went to the cashier for a tub of two-pence pieces.

'I'm going to win this diamond ring for you,' he announced. 'Only the best jewels for my new lady.'

She laughed and exclaimed as he fed coin after coin

into the machine, groaning with mock despair as the ring teetered ever closer to the edge, yet still hung on without falling. She wanted that gimcrack ring as much as if it were a real diamond they were playing for. It might only be glass and cheap base metal, yet this ring felt more precious than Marty's signet ring or Leo's silver dolphin; it came from the best place of all, and it shone brighter than any star. When it finally clattered into the tray with a fistful of two-pence pieces, they both shouted with delight, and Jake scooped it up and told her to hold out her hand. He placed it slowly and carefully on her little finger and then looked up at her.

'Always remember today, Kara.'

She felt dizzy, breathless, and inside her head the clamour of the machines, the music, the shrieks of the children, suddenly gave way to a moment of silence.

'What did you say?'

Jake kissed her forehead. 'I said, always remember today.'

'Someone else said that to me once,' she said. 'The exact same words.'

Her right hand automatically reached for her left wrist to finger the olive worry beads. Then she remembered they weren't there. That Leo had betrayed her.

'Well he couldn't possibly have been as handsome as me,' he said, laughing. 'Come on, let's go and get fish and chips.'

When they sat on the sea wall throwing their last chips to the gulls, she felt tears well up. The day was so perfect. For a few hours she had forgotten she'd lost the friendship and love of everyone she cared about, that she didn't know how to get any of it back.

'What is it, Kara? What's wrong?'

'It's . . . I don't know – it's everything. I haven't had a day like this since I can remember – a day where everything is so good, so right, where the goodness and the rightness of it just fill me up until I'm about to burst. But yesterday I upset my mam – she's got this new boyfriend and I fell out with him. I'm not sure about him, but I know I should be kinder to her and give him a chance. And then there's Lou, my best friend – or she was my best friend until the dance. She told me some home truths that I didn't want to hear. And I was cruel to my ex-boyfriend – Marty – I should see him and explain properly, but I can't face it. And then there's Leo. But forget him, I've already realised he doesn't really matter . . .'

'I'm sure we can put it all right, Kara. As instructed, I've already forgotten Leo, whoever he is – was – and it sounds like you aren't far behind me. I know that when you're ready you'll find you can apologise to Marty. He might not forgive you, and you can't undo what's done, but you can make him feel better by letting him know that it was all about you and not about him. And Louise and your mam love you, they'll be okay.'

'But . . .'

He put his finger to her lips. 'No. There's no "but" about it. Come on, we're going to walk down to the pub now for a pint, and we'll work out how to put it all right.'

FOURTEEN

When Jake went out for milk the next day, Kara decided to take a quick look round upstairs.

Her old room was empty, the walls painted a plain cream, but the window seat that Da had built for her was still there. When she was a baby the room had been magical. There was a mobile fashioned from delicate shells and sea glass, pictures of ships and seabirds which Da framed with driftwood. He foraged in junk shops, bought a vase in the shape of a dolphin, Murano glass paperweights filled with tiny neon tetra fish, a pottery lighthouse, a mermaid bedside lamp, and a clock like a ship's wheel.

The room echoed now, filled with ghosts.

She went back up to the attic and slipped on her swimming costume underneath her jeans and T-shirt. She would swim until those spirits disappeared.

As she passed her old room on the way down she suddenly remembered something. She went back in and knelt down on the floor, slid her hand along the front panel of the window seat and pressed the catch of the secret compartment. To her delight it sprung open, just as before. Inside, she found the component parts of her unfinished paper angelfish, and Sakara's wings, carefully rolled up and tied with the blue ribbons. She lifted them out and unrolled them: the wide wingspan of her grief.

Outside the window, the water was far out at low tide, the beach empty save for a dog walker. A lone fishing boat interrupted the straight line of the horizon, and Kara imagined Da out on the trawler, a flock of gulls circling overhead.

When Jake came back he found her upstairs, looking out across the bay with tears in her eyes.

'Kara?' He walked across to the window seat and sat at the other end, picking up one of the wings and holding it against the light. 'These are beautiful,' he said. 'Where did you find them?'

'They're mine,' she said. 'My da made them for me when I was six years old. They're Sakara's wings.'

'Sakara, the sea sprite? "The guardian of the northernmost sea, where the cold fish shiver".'

'Wow! You know the book?'

'I loved that book when I was a child! The idea that you could pass through a secret portal to another underwater world, to the other side of the sea.'

He picked up the paper angelfish and carefully unrolled it, sending a confetti of dry flower petals fluttering across the floor. Kara saw that it was a sad thing: no fins, no wings, neither fish nor angel. It could neither fly nor swim, steer nor soar. She had never attached the layer of card and the feathers, because Da hadn't brought the glue home that night.

'What about the fish, Kara? This strange fish without fins?'

'We were making the angelfish together, Da and I, the day before he was lost at sea. It's half-fish, half-angel.'

'I'm being slow to catch on, aren't I? You didn't bring these with you, they were already here in this room. So this was your house, Kara? Why didn't I realise before?' Are you the girl who—'

'The girl who what?' she interrupted. 'The girl who thought she could walk on water, who could dive beneath the waves and fetch her father back to shore? The girl who everyone thought was a little mad?'

Jake shook his head. 'I wasn't around then,' he said. 'I only know that a fisherman who lived here was lost at sea, and the body was never found, that no one knew what had really happened . . .' He paused.

'And?' she said.

'What?'

'You were going to say something else. I never really heard or understood the gossip when I was a child – my mother and I have never talked about it. Yet I know what everyone thought. That he went away with Lola Armitage. But it wasn't true. My father would never have done that to us. To me. I know that.'

He shook his head again. 'I wasn't going to say that. I've never heard of Lola Armitage. But I did hear that the fisherman's daughter tried to drown herself.'

He paused, but Kara stayed silent.

'I know how hard it is to grieve and hope at the same time. The world and every last thing in it stay exactly the same: the tide still turns, the sun shines as brightly as before. The sameness of it all is brutal, the hardest thing to bear. Everyone carries on as though nothing has happened, you want to shake them, to shout at them in the street. All the people that still have their fathers, their mothers, their brothers . . .'

Kara watched the dog on the beach as he raced after a neon-bright tennis ball, his tail curled up in a perfect circle.

'How can you really know what it's like for me though, Jake? Louise told me you lost your brother in a car accident. So you know he's dead, you have closure, finality. You know for certain he didn't betray you.'

She didn't turn to look at him, but carried on staring out to sea as she talked.

'The night before Da's accident he told me that Siberian cranes migrate to Iran or China every winter – a round trip of thousands of miles. When they return in the spring they make their nests in the same place as the previous year, with the same mate. Sometimes they may not have migrated together, yet they'll always find each other again and rear more chicks. Most pairs will stay faithful for their entire lives. I asked him what happens when one of them waits and the other doesn't return? They would never know why their mate hadn't come back – I couldn't bear the thought of their sadness, of them hoping and waiting. Da didn't answer me at first. He stood up and rested his hand gently on the top of my head, looked out through the window at the darkening sky, then quoted two lines of poetry I'd never heard before:

"The snow cranes are ready to fly south again
with all our squandered beauty stowed beneath
their wings."

'It was as though he'd forgotten I was there for a moment. I reached up for his hand, he looked down at me then and answered my question.

"'That's the price of love, Kara."

'And since he went missing I've been like the lone snow crane I used to imagine, waiting for him to return. Never really knowing the truth.'

106

'And your mam too. It must've been hard for her?'

'Yes, it was – it still is I guess. As a child I was too selfish to see that. I know I haven't always been as kind to her as I could have been.'

'What happened on the night of the accident?'

'I was waiting for Da to arrive home with the glue to finish making my angelfish. I thought he must be doing something in the boathouse and have forgotten the time. I could just make out the shed from the landing window, and I was sure I could see a faint glow coming from the skylight. I asked Mam if I could go and fetch him. It was only six o'clock, but I could feel the evening drawing in, the cold of it coming off the sea. When I got near to the boathouse I realised the light I'd seen had been the setting sun glinting on the glass. I could see Da's motorbike was parked around the side, yet the door was locked. I knocked and shouted for him, but it was silent inside. The window was too high up for me to see in, and I couldn't find anything tall enough to stand on. I knocked again and waited, then went round to try the double doors at the front. They were locked too, but I could see through the keyhole, and even in the half-light of dusk I could tell that the shed was empty. I thought Da must have gone out in the coble to check his lobster pots. I looked out to sea, but there were no boats in sight save for a container ship far out on the horizon.

'Mam called the coastguard and it was two hours later when the lifeboat returned, towing Da's boat in its wake. The coble was undamaged, found empty and drifting, out of fuel. Divers went down, but Da's body was never found. There was speculation, but without a body it could only be concluded it was an accident, that he'd slipped overboard and hadn't been able to make it back onto the boat.'

'And what about the woman you mentioned?'

'No one remembers seeing Lola again after that night. There was talk that she'd left Elmwick in a hurry to look after her ill mother, but no one really knew. So someone sparked a rumour, said Da had faked his own death, that he'd run off with Lola. Her family came from somewhere down south, and she'd made no real friends here, so we never found out the truth. But I know the truth. I know Da would never have done that to us.'

Kara reached in her bag and showed Jake the photo of her and Da stood by the Canny Lass. It was her favourite photo of Da, taken the day she'd helped him re-paint the name on the boat's prow. He was standing behind her, his hands loosely resting on her shoulders, and she was reaching up with both skinny arms to clasp hold of his fingers. The sun was in their eyes and they were both grinning wildly. There was a smudge of red paint on Da's face where he'd wiped his hand across his forehead.

Jake stared at it for a long time.

'What happened to the Canny Lass?' he asked.

'She was sold straight away. It was as though Mam couldn't bear to see her again.'

He handed the photo back to her, stared out at the water and didn't answer straight away. When he spoke, his voice was urgent and animated in a way she hadn't heard before. As though he was suddenly hopeful, confident, even quietly excited.

'I think you should come with me to Ravengrove tomorrow, Kara. I want to show you my home village, and I've got an idea about something that might help you find closure. Will you trust me?'

She nodded. What did she have to lose?

FIFTEEN

Kara had never been to Ravengrove, she only knew of its reputation. It was pirate country, the home of smugglers, the wild wild west of the north-east coast, a place where outsiders felt unwelcome, where every young lad could sail and fish, fight and shoot. The steelworks may have paid the villagers' wages, yet the sea still ruled everything.

Jake pulled up at the bottom of the village by the raggle-taggle line of boat sheds. Heads turned as Kara took off her helmet, yet no one spoke until Jake gave the men a curt nod of his head. The coble landing was strewn with battered boats, the young men sprawled out on them with cigarettes dangling from the corners of their mouths, crushed beer cans strewn in the rutted couch grass.

The women of the village were nowhere to be seen and the men eyed Kara with suspicion. Jake had already told her that most of them worked the nightshift in the steelworks, still went fishing most days too, sometimes taking their shotguns to the fields to shoot rabbits and pigeons.

Kara asked about the women, was surprised when Jake told her that Ravengrove was a matriarchal society, that the women ruled the roost with a rod of iron. They took no orders from their husbands and sons, and their young daughters were sent down to the beach every day to fill sacks with sea coal and driftwood.

Despite the brightness of the day, the village seemed drained of colour. Kara felt as though she was watching an old black and white film, as far removed from the lights of Hayborough as could be imagined.

They walked over to a terrace of pebble-dashed houses, stopped outside the last cottage in the row, paint peeling, the small front yard filled with old nets, rusting tools, lengths of sea-worn wood.

Jake opened the door into a dark, narrow hallway. Kara could hear voices – an argument – coming from the kitchen. Jake laughed at her worried face.

'That's just my da and his sister. They're always like that.'

Kara thought of her and Mam, the peace of the house, the radio playing quietly in the background.

'What about your mam?'

'My mother left us, Kara. That's why I understand what it's like not to have closure. It's not only my brother I lost. We're all still waiting for Mam to return. She walked out on us when I was four years old, yet I'll never stop hoping.'

'Do you look for her wherever you go? I look for Da, but I only ever see Lola -- I see Lola everywhere.'

'Yes, I look for Mam in shops, on the beach, in the pub, walking along the pier, sat in bus windows. I imagine bumping into her one day, try to think what I'd say to her. But I have no real idea what I would say. She's hardly real any more, I'm no longer angry with her. When I was a kid I had to fill myself with grit and surround myself with steel to get by. Round here, you want to make sure no one sees any weakness – that they only know the hard exterior. My da is the same way too, he hasn't learned to let go of it yet.'

The kitchen door opened and Jake's da came out. He nodded to Kara, gave her a quick glance up and down, then turned to his son.

'I got the key for you. Mind you bring it back in an hour or two.'

They went back outside, Kara blinking at the sudden brightness after the dim interior.

'Come on,' said Jake, 'I've something to show you.'

As they walked back down to the sheds, Kara noticed a young boy on the beach wearing a navy-blue suit and a shirt and tie. He looked incongruous, uncomfortable, among the broken lobster pots and the lads in their fishing sweaters and overalls. He stood with his hands in his pockets, watching an older boy hooking a boat and trailer onto a tractor.

'That's Sonny Rowe,' said Jake. 'His father was drowned just a couple of weeks ago. His family went out to sea last week to honour the Ravengrove tradition. The ritual of the seventh tide. It's believed that sailors' souls are trapped in sea glass. When a fisherman is lost, we collect glass washed up on the beach by the seventh tide after the death. The family tie it inside a handkerchief or a scarf that belonged to the deceased and take it back out to sea. Then they kiss the bundle and cast it back into the water. Only then can the soul be released, and the family begin to let out their grief.'

'So that's why people from here got the nickname "seveners"? My da told me that sea glass held the souls of sailors too. But he believed that if we find glass that matches the colour of a sailor's eyes then they'll be returned to the land. I always thought it was something he made up especially for me, but maybe your village tradition is where the idea came from. I like the ritual of the seventh tide; it makes sense, there would be a comfort in it. Some kind of closure.'

Jake nodded. 'Some of our traditions are a little more frowned upon by those who don't understand this village. Sonny is here today in his Sunday best, ready to go out to sea with his elder brother. If the man of the house is lost at sea then the family like to send the younger sons straight out – to make sure they don't become afraid of the water. They always dress up, wear their Sunday best, as a symbol of the ritual's importance and as a mark of respect to the sea. There's too many round here who think they own the sea, who think they can conquer the waves, even though all the evidence proves them wrong. And the less respect they have for the water, the less respect it will have for them.'

Kara shivered. 'I can see that some people would think it callous to send a young boy out on a small boat like that when his da's ashes are scarcely cold. I wasn't much older than Sonny when I nearly drowned. It was the day I found out my mam had sold the house. I wanted to stay by the sea in Elmwick, where I felt close to Da. So I went to find him.'

'What happened?'

'I was spotted by a dog walker on the pier. He threw a life ring and managed to pull me in to the steps.'

Jake stopped outside the last boat shed and put the key in the lock.

'You're not going to take me out on a boat because you think it will help me get over Da?'

He shook his head. 'This is better than that, Kara.'

He turned the huge key in the old doors and pushed them back. In the half-gloom she saw a small coble, painted a bright cobalt blue like the Canny Lass. She paused for a moment, turned to look at Jake.

'No? How could . . .?'

He flicked on the light and she saw the name on the prow, painted in yellow, shadowed in red, just as it had always been.

'It was Denny Blake who bought her, but he died in a trawling accident not six months later. He had no sons, only girls, and his wife has kept the boat here ever since. A rumour went around that she was cursed, so no one wanted to buy her. When I saw your photo I realised it was the same boat.'

Kara saw the ladder propped up near the stern of the coble.

'Can I go up on deck?'

'Of course, that's why I brought you here. I'm going to leave you on your own for a while – if you want me to? I thought that's what you'd prefer?'

He pulled the doors closed behind her, and she stood in the silence, disturbed dust motes dancing in the dull light from the single bulb. Kara traced her finger along the hull's peeling paintwork as she walked round to where the ladder was propped against the blue planks.

The boat was almost empty, just a coil of rope on the deck and the old Persian carpet, mildewed and salt-stained, inside the tiny cabin.

Yet she found herself lifting up seats, scouring the lockers, desperately seeking some sign, something to reveal what had happened that night, what Da had been thinking, anything to prove beyond doubt that he'd meant to come home. In the last of the lockers she found the old canvas knapsack he'd used for carrying his lunch. The empty coffee flask was there, still intact, and as she held it in her hands she staggered under the weight of the sadness it held, of its everyday ordinariness, of its familiarity. The faded yellow flask with the tiny chip in the cup, the solid feel of the lid as she unscrewed it. She sank to her knees on the deck, cradling it in her arms, rocking back and forth, crying all the tears she'd held back for so long, all the tears that had been frozen inside her.

When she heard Jake calling her name, she grasped the side of the boat and hauled herself up. As she opened the knapsack to put the flask back, she heard a rattle in the bottom. She reached inside, her hand closing around a small smooth tube and a flat stone – it was a brand-new tube of superglue and the pebble Da had promised to carry with him wherever he went until the end of time. She rubbed it clean between her finger and thumb, the colours as bright and true as ever, and she could hear Da's voice.

'The elves will polish your stone until it shines.'

She held it tightly in her palm and sank back down to the deck.

'Kara? Are you okay? Have you found anything?'

She looked down at Jake, her face streaked with tears and dirt.

'I've found everything I need.'

SIXTEEN

When they arrived back at the cottage, Kara didn't go inside, she told Jake she needed to think for a while. She sat on the garden wall and pulled the amber sea glass from her jeans pocket, turning it around in her hand with the varnished stone. She knew what she had to do. She turned to see if Jake was watching her from the window, and when she was sure he'd gone upstairs she placed Da's knapsack inside the porch and walked down the beach without a backward glance.

She'd never believed Da had left with Lola, and now she was sure. She knew she would never find out exactly what happened out there on the Canny Lass, yet she was certain he'd never planned to leave her and Mam, that he'd always intended to come home that night.

Da was still out at sea, waiting for her.

The sea whispered louder to Kara here than it did in Hayborough. In the town, it was often drowned out by the clamour of amusement arcades, day-trippers and children's laughter, but in Elmwick the sound of the waves became Da's voice, relentlessly drawing Kara towards the water.

She kicked off her shoes at the shoreline, not even bothering to undress, bracing herself against the cold as she walked into the shallows. She heard Jake calling her from the kitchen window and for a moment she turned round. They were so similar in a way. She knew he understood her, that he was wise beyond his years, yet she also knew he couldn't save her. She could only save herself.

She clutched the sea glass and the stone tightly, holding one in each hand, her arms outstretched as though offering gifts to some unseen sea god. She waded in, deeper and deeper, thrusting her hips against the solid wall of water. But the sea didn't want her. It argued with her, pushed her away, and she could hear Da's voice telling her to go back, go back, go back. The currents tugged at her ankles, tried to pull her over, turn her round, so she would wash up back on the shore.

A seagull soared above her, brilliant white against the summer sky, and she thought of the angel wings spread out on the window seat, of Da twisting the thin wire around the delicate feathers. She no longer believed in heaven or sea sprites, yet she was finally ready to use her wings. The world was a strange sea waiting to be explored. She could go to London, she could return to Elmwick. She could be half-fish, half-angel. She could fly, she could swim, she didn't have to settle for one or the other.

Kara finally understood that grief and love were things outside her control; that they had their own lives. You couldn't choose who or why or when, or decide how long they would last or when to say enough was enough. They would play out in their own time.

She looked back to the shore, saw Jake wading into the shallows, both arms raised, waving, shouting. Behind him, on the sea wall, was a woman with red hair, shading her eyes with her hand, a dog running in circles around her. It was Mam and Pilot.

Kara turned around again to face the horizon, a thin

ribbon of pink sky at the rim of the earth. Another day, another turn of the planet, another cycle of tides. The pull and push, the ebb and flow, the give and take. Not seven, but thousands of tides since Da had drowned, yet she could still do this last thing for him. Kara stepped farther out, pushing hard against the water, then lifted her arms clear of the waves. She kissed the glass and the pebble in turn, tasted salt on her lips as she hurled them with all her strength, casting them far out into the northernmost sea, where the cold fish shiver.

Acknowledgements

I'm incredibly grateful to Consuelo Rivera-Fuentes and the team at Victorina Press for making this book happen, to Triona Walsh for her cover design, to Helen Mayes for her friendship and support through every draft, and huge thanks (as always) to the long-suffering Mr L.

About the Author

Amanda Huggins is the author of three collections of short fiction – *Brightly Coloured Horses, Separated From the Sea* and *Scratched Enamel Heart.* She has also published a poetry collection, *The Collective Nouns for Birds*, which won the 2020 Saboteur Award for Best Poetry Pamphlet.

She has been placed and listed in numerous competitions including Fish, Bridport, Bath, the Alpine Fellowship Writing Award and the Colm Toibin International Short Story Award. In 2018 her story 'Red' was a finalist in the Costa Short Story Award. Her travel writing has also won several prizes, notably the BGTW New Travel Writer of the Year in 2014, and she has twice been a finalist in the Bradt Guides New Travel Writer Award.

Amanda grew up on the North Yorkshire coast, moved to London in the 1990s, and now lives in West Yorkshire.